Anna's Story

WOMAN OF THE SECRET PLACE

CAROL ANDERSON

Ark House Press
arkhousepress.com

Cataloguing in Publication Data:
Title: Anna's Story
ISBN: 978-0-6455535-2-9 (pbk)
Subjects: Fiction

Design by initiateagency.com

PERSONAL TESTIMONIES

A beautifully written story weaving together Old Testaments prophesies with New Testament events. Such a personal journey portraying the timeless plans of God our Father and His Sacrificial Love, Thanks for the privilege of reading it.

Jayne

Thank you for letting me read your great book, I really enjoyed it. It gave me a new creative perspective to view the story and I discovered some treasures in there too. I hope you can have it published and share it with many more people.

Regards Robert

I have wept through your book; it has touched me in such a deep way. It has been about Him, not us. We love Him, because He first loved us.
Thank you for allowing me to read it. It is all about intimacy with Him.

Bless you Brenda

I was blessed to read your story of Anna. It is very precious, and it touched my heart. I saw you often when you wrote of Anna.
We can learn much and be inspired by Anna's relationship with her Lord.
So very beautiful.

Love Robyn

Thank you so much for allowing me to read your amazing God given story. I believe it is all you and your heart full of love just pouring out. Your desire to be with The Lord and draw us as close as possible. It is so beautiful, and I enjoyed it so much. (Gloria my sister told me it was just a beautiful story, and she would love to meet the writer one day. (She will – in heaven).

Love Janette

Amazing read! It made me cry 3 times. You have to get this published – it is truly a divine walk of inspiration!

Nigel

May the doorways of heaven be opened up to get this precious book published. Anointed to heal, anointed to bring revelation and understanding. A book that drips with the intimacy of God.

As I was reading this book, I quickly discovered it was not just a story but an experience with my heavenly Father. For me it was a journey of His heart drawing me into Him. His healing power washing over me as the pages drew out pain that had been hidden deep below.

The author of this book is a precious vessel that carries the intimacy of God in her Spirit. That very spirit flows through this book as you read it.

Rea

This book is dedicated entirely with love and thanks to The One True and Living God and The Son whom He sent and Lovely Holy Spirit.

It is You who gave me a gift to read and write- and a passion for Your Word – You taught me…. Thank You.

I have not always journeyed well but always – You picked me up and have been all things for me – with Your constant Love.

Anna's Story was written at least ten years ago – and though many read the manuscript, I never knew how to publish.

It is in Your Time Now… You brought along all the people it would take to give this book wings. I thank You because You orchestrated it all. May It always be All for Your Glory!!!

Though I have not seen You I love You and though I do not see You now – I believe in You and greatly rejoice with joy inexpressible and full of Glory.

But my heart says, "Seek His face" "Your Beautiful Face I will seek!"

My heartfelt thanks
to my very special friends Wendy and Owen from the moment we met – God was always on your hearts and shared with such wisdom and love- you both inspire me … you walk the pages of The Word

To my beautiful Spiritual son and daughter
Dave and Breie
I love you both so much and your precious daughters
Teeghan and Baby Peace I love this gift of family love mumma Carol

Special love and thanks for Marilyn for her constant love, joy and peace and all the millions of things she does

Matthew breaking open The Word of God with you was always better than the meal itself, and our meals were amazing- so anointed

Lorna, truly a woman who loves the Lord, loves the Word and reads it always, loves great teachings and preaching – loves to wake up and sing and pray every day, a gift and a blessing to the church. Such a beautiful friend to me – love you

Kareena my Dear friend you just keep singing and shining no matter what season we are in. Thank you for this precious friendship

A personal note of heartfelt thanks to James and Nicole at Ark House publishing – you brought this to life with the gifts on your lives. You gave it wings and were so encouraging and wonderfully creative and patient.

CONTENTS

CHAPTER 1

The most powerful memory Anna held onto was that moment when she knew, her beloved husband of only seven short years had died.

Somehow, the Holy God of Israel had spoken into her heart that day, and she ran, the child - woman - she was, to the temple, knowing it would be too late.

When she finally made it panting and out of breath, instinctively she ran to the spot that they had laid him on the tiled floor.

Anna the daughter of Phanuel of the tribe of Asher, drew in a deep breath as she knelt on the tiled floor, she heard in her heart, her father speaks those words that Moses had spoken to the tribes- "About Asher", he said "Most blessed of sons is Asher- let him be favoured by his brothers and let him bathe his feet in oil. The bolts of your gates will be iron and bronze and your strength will equal your days."

She watched her lifeless husband and could hear him as he had so many times in the past, continue the scripture. "There is no one like the God of Jeshurun who rides on the heavens to help you and on the clouds in His Majesty."

"The Eternal God is your refuge," Anna cried falling deeply in her brokenness upon her husband's chest.

She lay there in the silence so long clinging to him, the lights of the candles burned dimly, and suddenly a gentle breeze blew across her face. Peace entered her heart as she arose knowing what was required of her.

Those were dark days every one of them. A cloud hung over her, so low reminding her she was in the valley of the shadow of death. It was such a real place- it had its own fragrance. It was a heavy place filled with doubt and endless grief and anger, what if's and why's.

She would wake constantly through the nights and each time remember "He was gone, and he was gone forever," and then she would cry.

For seven days as is the custom a family member sat with her, never talking, all the pressure was off, they just sat quietly together in their aloneness.

Anna was twenty-one the first time she cried out to the Living God to take her home. Always her angry outbursts were met by His silence. It was in this place that was so full of tears and memories and all the other unseen emotions that a new moulding and shaping began, she fought it every step of the way.

The days passed slowly and the nights even slower, the barrage of the women's chatter never ceased. She knew what they were thinking these women some old and widowed themselves, others were married, and their husbands were busy, so their wives made themselves busier going from house-to-house gossiping. As hard as it was to listen to - even harder was knowing what they were saying just out of ear shot.

Anna was far too young to receive any help at all, she was childless so that left her in the care of her father to provide all her needs. And what made it so much worse, was she was beautiful.

Anna knew it was better for the unmarried and the widows to stay unmarried but if they can't control themselves, they should marry, for it is better to marry than burn with passion.

Her passion had died, all that remained was an empty shell. "Never! she vowed in her bitterness "Never will I marry again- nor will I love another man again."

The gossip continued every time she would leave her father's house- eyes would follow her and whisperings would be on the wind with fingers pointing. Such cruelty those first few months.

Anna shared none of what she was going through with anyone but the Living God and though she never heard Him, He became someone she could confide in - and cry with and walk with and on the rare occasion- smile with.

CHAPTER 2

The First Kiss

It was almost a full three months since her husband had died and his birthday was causing such pain in her heart that she felt the place she would feel nearer to him would be in the temple that he had loved so much. So, on that very day she found herself picking flowers and with veil pulled low over her face, hiding so much, she walked back into the temple.

It was unusually quiet, as she felt drawn back to the place on the tiles where she had last held her husband. She lay the flowers where his body would have been. She lay there rocking with eyes closed and allowed her tears and frustration and all that was within her to be poured out.

A gentle breeze blew across her face causing her veil to feel like a kiss upon her lips. Anna smiled and lay herself down on the tiled floors so cold and hard. She lifted the veil and felt such indescribable Peace. "This is where I belong," she declared out loud, unaware that anyone but the Holy God had heard.

She had laid there for so long that as she went to arise, she was stiff and sore, but strangely refreshed. This was her turning point, the first time she had awoken after sleep without her inner voice reminding her 'And he's gone, and he's gone forever.'

Candles were burning and the stillness of the room brought such comfort. It was then she remembered the breeze on her face, it didn't frighten her, she was in a Holy Temple and The Most High God who heard her prayer was in this place.

'Was that You?' she wondered to herself.

Day after day Anna found her way to the temple always, she would pick flowers on her way, always heading to the same place on the floor, always wearing her widow's clothes.

Sometimes she just sat in the silence, other times grief would overwhelm her again and she would just cry. But more and more she began to talk to the Most High God...

One day as she sat in the silence, she heard a voice and though she looked around there was no one. And then it came again from deep within her.

"Sing to Me."

Anna laughed. It was Him finally speaking to her, just like He had to Samuel.

"Sing what?" She laughed.

Suddenly the Song of Moses and Miriam sprang into her heart as she opened her mouth. The song her father and her late husband had sang with her came joyously out.

"I will sing to the Lord for He is Highly exalted, the horse and its rider He has hurled into the sea. The Lord is my strength and my song. He has become my salvation. He is my God, and I will praise Him, my father's God, and I will exalt Him."

"You made me laugh," Anna said out loud forgetting herself for that moment that here she was a bereaved very young woman talking with The Holy God of Israel.

"And," She said "You made Sarah laugh as well, didn't you? Only she was too afraid to admit it to You."

Anna sat crossed legged on the floor with a hidden cushion under her robe to save herself a numb bottom. Another secret she shared with The Most High God and laughed quietly with what suddenly seemed like a new friend.

Days flowed into weeks - then weeks to months and all Anna yearned for was to be in the temple. It was no longer about her memories of her husband, what she had found now was far beyond what even her father and her husband had talked about.

From the moment she woke all she found herself longing for above everything, was to be in His Presence in His Temple. She would go without meals just because she couldn't drag herself away from Him.

The whisperings of the women changed, no longer was it about her as a widow, it was quite amusing to her now as they referred to her as this "Very Holy Woman -fasting and praying- she never leaves the temple," she heard them say of her.

"If only they knew," she thought. Sometimes in a month a young woman is considered unclean, and she would find herself sleeping at her father's house. Her days walking and exploring quite often now she would take this treasured walk and cross the Kidron Valley to the Mount of Olives and deep unexplained stirrings within her would draw her to the garden of

Gethsemane. And she would well up with unexplained tears so powerful that she would end up face down in the dirt, barely able to breathe.

But a woman of prayer, that made her laugh, as far as she understood not one prayer had she uttered. She talked to Him and laughed and sang to Him, but she never asked for anything for herself or anyone. This was enough!

Nothing prepared Anna for the shock news her father imparted to her as she crept into the house long after dark.

"Sit down Anna your father has much I have to say to you."

Anna searched her father's face looking for a clue as to what he was going to say that was so serious.

"Anna please sit, this, well this is quite difficult to say."

"Father what whatever it is, it will be alright."

"You know the widow of James - Miriam the one who's been on her own for,"

"Father what, what has she said, I haven't done anything, please believe me," Anna cried falling on her knees in front of her father.

"Anna, my precious Anna," Her father drew in breath not knowing how to say what was on his heart.

"Anna I am to marry her." There it was out- he waited and not a word was spoken.

"We are both old Anna both widows, please understand."

Anna was stunned after all these years her father was going to invite another woman into their home.

"Anna, I think it best if you think about the same, there has been a suitor, he has seen and heard you at the temple. He has come quite frequently of late asking for you."

Anna's mind was whirling her father marrying and to even contemplate her marrying when he knew how she felt, and who was this watching her in the temple?

"Anna I will no longer be able to take care of all your needs as I will have a wife now to take care of. It's for the best don't you see."

Anna ran blindly out of her father's house and into the one place she felt safe.

"The Lord is my Shepherd I shall not be in want, He makes me lay down in green pastures," tears stinging her face as she ran faster and faster speaking out her favorite Psalm.

"He leads me beside quiet waters, He restores my soul - He guides me in paths of righteousness for His Name's sake- Even though I walk through the valley of the shadow of death...."

Anna looked up at the sky - the blackness was full of stars "The heavens declare the Glory of God."

She was so determined to make it to the temple.

"You are my help,"

"I will fear no evil, You are with me, Your rod and Your staff they comfort me."

"You prepare a table before me in the presence of my enemies."

"You anoint my head with oil- my cup overflows."

Anna raced to her spot on the tiled floor laying herself down prostrate before the Holy God of Israel.

"Surely goodness and love will follow me all the days of my life."

She cried so hard, fear, the unknown came crashing in on her and with all her strength she whispered her most powerful prayer.

"And I will dwell in the house of the Lord forever!"

A great weight seemed to be upon her, and a light seemed to be shining from within her and she knew without a doubt, that it was the glorious weighty presence of Jehovah.

Tears silent and beautiful cascaded down her face as she knew He had answered her prayer.

"I belong here, this is where I belong!" "Thank you, Lord." Anna cried out.

And over and over Anna spoke His Name and each time she did, He touched her afresh.

In the morning without a word spoken a bowl of food was laid before her. She smiled knowing her Lord had provided. Throughout the day a woman of great age took her by the hand and led her to a section of the temple she had never been, there was a bowl of fresh water and very simple and wonderful things were before her.

And then her eyes became accustomed to the dimness of the room, and she noticed the prayer shawl folded neatly and her heart responded to the gift of great value by overflowing in tears. There were two lamps burning their wicks were trimmed, and their oil was full.

The older woman had silently withdrawn from the room and left Anna there overwhelmed with the tenderness of her Lord.

More and more she found herself quite at ease on her face laying prostrate before Him on the floor.

"Thank you, my Lord."

Slowly she made her way to her knees and picked up the precious prayer shawl and draped it around herself.

In the silence deep within, Anna heard that still soft voice speak to her, before she entered into the stillness of His Presence. "I Am Your Father."

CHAPTER 3

Temptation

Just after the first anniversary of her husband's death, Anna's relationship with her Lord changed- it deepened as He made her hunger for Him and Him alone.

He woke her one morning before the dawn and whispered that He loved her with an everlasting love and that He had drawn her with loving kindness, but it was His next words that went into the core of her being.

"I your God am a Jealous God."

Anna arose abruptly from her bed and made her way to the place on the tiles, her prayer shawl wrapped around her as if it was Him. She lay herself down and began to sing to Him, but something was wrong, and she could sense it.

All day Anna talked to her Lord, she prayed His Word and sang. She lay in the silence, but not once did she feel a stir in her heart. She never sensed Him draw near.

In her anguish she knelt and cried "Father what have I done?" But it was only silence.

"Forgive me- Father have I said something - done something - have I grieved You- O Father tell me?"

The hours were becoming unbearable without Him, she knew He would never leave her nor forsake her, but she knew that He had drawn away.

In her sadness and brokenness, she neither ate nor slept, she wept and cried out for Him but day after day, week after week she remained seeking Him with all her heart, her soul and her mind but she found Him not.

It was in this weakened place where she was desperate that temptation came to her, she was so lonely and after clinging to the silence in the room the voice that broke her despair entered.

Luke had watched Anna from a distance for a year now waiting for her to cease grieving her husband, but of late instead of blossoming she was more broken hearted.

He walked across the room and knelt on the floor a comfortable distance from her and began to pray.

It was lovely to hear a man's voice, it was like rain falling on a dry and thirsty land and as he prayed the scriptures, she drank deeply. Not once in that first week, did she lift her eyes to see him, but strangely her sadness was replaced by a new desire.

She found herself looking forward to him coming to meet with her on the tiles. When she left in the evenings now for refreshing sleep her mind wandered and she thought of him and awoke to thoughts of him.

When the whole day had passed, and he had not come she found herself disappointed until she heard his footsteps drawing near. She smiled and waited on him to speak, but he sat and all she heard was him breathing.

She lifted her head ever so slightly and stole a glance at the man beside her. He smiled as did she, he was very beautiful and for the first time since her husband's death she looked at another man- really looked at him. "Come" he said, "to the gates, I have something for you."

Luke stood up to leave and Anna made her way to her feet.

It was a beautiful night the moon was full providing plenty of light. Anna followed one small pace behind this man from the temple. It felt so natural to be walking with this man. He stopped at the gate and reached for a bag that had been hidden.

Anna watched with such curiosity as he pulled bread from his bag, it must have been just freshly baked with leaven in it and had risen and the aroma was mouthwatering. He motioned for her to sit right there by the gate and pulled a wine skin from his bag.

He broke the bread and reached over to give her some and she hesitated. "Take" He said, "and eat."

Anna rose to her feet so abruptly that she knocked the bread out of his hand.

"No, I'll not eat of your bread." She ran back into her room, numb.

"Lord" She cried "I'm sorry all I want is You!"

Still the silence remained, no sooner had she got through her disappointment in herself at being led away from her Lord so easily than another temptation came.

Anna's father sent word to her on the break of day to come at once to the house. The young man who brought the message had no more to impart so Anna as usual took time to pray and sing to her Lord. Still the silence remained- the joy that she used to feel as He drew near was missing. "Lord" She cried "I'm going to my father's."

Anna walked into the morning air and breathed in deeply. "What a wonderful day." Flowers were appearing all over the earth and she really felt led to sing. Smiling and rejoicing as she walked along the path to her home.

"Anna almost opened the door and went racing in, but she thought it was right to call out first as for some time she had not seen her father and his new wife.

Miriam greeted her at the door with a warm embrace and Anna knew it was genuine.

Her father was sitting on the floor mending something as she walked through. His smile lit up the room. Standing to his feet, he rushed at his daughter with an enormous hug. Joyful tears ran down his face and onto hers.

"I have missed you precious Anna," He said lifting her off the ground like she was a child again.

"Goodness child don't you eat, the rumors are true then!" His voice was filled with concern.

Anna just kissed her father's face, the very scent of him was more than she could bare and broke down in his arms and sobbed.

Anna's father drew Miriam into his outstretched arm also and spoke lovingly to his daughter, still held in his embrace. Drawing his two women close against him.

"We have talked it through, and I have built another room onto the house for you. You are to stay with us, we are family."

Anna was shown to the newly acquired room and stared in amazement, it was everything she would have asked for. Her father knew her so well to have all those little needs met.

"Why father, why now?"

"I want you with me, is that not enough reason?"

Miriam stepped out of her husband's arms and spoke so softly taking Anna's hand in her own.

"Anna, we hear how little you have, word has reached us and the loneliness you suffer, and our hearts are breaking because our joy has brought you such sorrow. We thought you would marry again not hide yourself away in the temple. You're a beautiful young woman- temple life is no life for you. Look around you, this can all be yours. Please come back."

Anna's eyes scanned the room as in her mind she compared what she had in her tiny room in the temple. The beauty displayed in this room was overwhelming. She walked over to the bed and sat on the softness of the mattress and picked up the bright new robe draped across the stool.

"Father, Miriam,"

"It's all so -so much."

Just having her father's arms around her - to feel his touch, to hear his words.

"I've missed you," She sighed, "But I don't want you to be sorry for me. I want you to be happy for me." Anna stepped out of their embrace to stand alone and gather her thoughts.

"Father, I have found Him, He meets with me in the temple. I cannot leave, I love Him."

"Anna sweet, sweet Anna, He is God, not a playmate. You need a friend; you need your family, and you need to eat. Come home and we will take care of you." His voice wavered, his confusion at hearing his daughter speak so, was unnerving him. Tears formed in his eyes, he tried desperately to hide.

"Father, I belong in the temple," and with a confidence she did not feel she turned first to her father and then to Miriam and kissed them on their cheeks and turned and walked away.

"I love you father, Miriam and I thank you, but what I have found is far greater than what you offer."

Anna made it as far as the path before the sting hit. It had been weeks since she had experienced His presence and there was no promise she would ever again, but she could not leave.

"All I want is You." A gentle breeze blew across her face, and she was reminded of Him. "Show me your beauty."

And as she turned her face there in the distance was the most beautiful flower. The very beautiful and fragrant "Rose of Sharon."

Anna had walked in grief before, she recognized it, not immediately at first but slowly her continued sadness, waiting on Him and wondering what she had done took her to a place in her heart she never thought she would enter again. There was a heaviness in her walk, a light had gone out of her eyes and no longer was she filled with tears, she was numb.

But even that place shifted so quickly for her as the months passed so far from His presence. Something new rose up in her as she made her way to the tiles.

An anger was brewing deep within because He was doing this to her. Because she wanted Him and loved Him above all else and her passion for Him spilled over, and in silence she screamed louder pouring out all her frustrations.

Anyone looking on would have seen a young woman sitting, rocking eyes closed, lips moving and thought she was deep in prayer. This was no prayer. Anna was giving her friend the Lord, the Living God, all her rage. She held nothing back until she was so exhausted that she fell on to the tiles and lay in the dimness, aware He had not come. He would never come.

Long before the sun rose Anna crawled herself off the floor, remorseful and bitter and more in love than ever. Her heart felt like it had been pierced through.

And she ran, she ran, and ran, and ran outside the temple, uncaring, unsure where she was headed. Just running to the gates of the city itself.

She ran along a path and looked up and saw the place she had only ever heard about.

Her father and her husband had both protected her from such a place. It was eerie and she wrapped her shawl so much tighter around herself.

There was a cross- the moonlight was just capturing it and it took all her strength to remain on her feet. Thankfully no one was on it, and for reasons she never understood she felt compelled to climb up the hill called Golgotha- The Place of the Skull.

None of what she did made sense to her, depression caused her to think and feel and behave in a way not like herself at all.

She stood in front of the cross as the moonlight shone upon her face and with arms outstretched, she lifted her eyes to the heavens and cried out. "Father forgive me."

The very same day Anna walked aimlessly, dusty and tired overcome and found herself looking into a pool of water. Men and women of all ages were laying on mats or sitting on the stairs. Mostly blind, some were lame, all of them needed healing and without thinking she stepped into the pool fully clothed and sunk down into the water.

She forgot to hold her breath and came up spluttering and caused such a commotion amongst those sitting there. She felt more awake as she stepped out of the pool, refreshed. The weight of her clothing made walking back to the temple seem longer and harder, people staired at her as she walked with her wet robes hanging against her skin.

The third temptation came in a most unexpected way. Anna had resigned herself to sitting in silence and walking alone through the Olive Grove. Hope deferred had made her heart sick. She felt like her lover had left her and remembered the wonderful Song of Solomon. She clung to what she could remember and wished that she could learn now.

The thought began to occur to her that maybe she in her grief over losing her husband had created a relationship with The Most High God. But as quickly as it came, she knew in all her heart it was real. He was real.

And then she would waiver and blame herself for His leaving. She continued to ask Him to forgive her, but silence remained.

It was on one of these treasured walks that she met a group of young people all her age. They were laughing and talking, and the young men were sharing things with the ladies.

Anna's ears burned as she listened. They had all been dancing at a wedding that last week and the joy was still alive in them. The men were jovial and grabbed the ladies by the hands and danced with them as they sang. They clapped their hands and made music, it was lighthearted and so much fun.

The lady who rested on the tree trunk noticed Anna and called out to her to come and join in. There was laughter and warmth in her voice, within moments they were all beckoning her to come.

Anna shied away and they refused to take No for an answer, one of the young men came up behind her and grabbed her hand, Anna froze.

"We won't bite you, come on let's dance, no one is watching," they said playfully.

And suddenly she had both hands held and they danced with her, laughing and jeering. They all introduced themselves and they invited her to come away with them. The young men had a boat, and they were all secretly going out on it. Three of the young ladies were married to the young men and though it could look untoward, they assured her no one would know.

To feel the sea air in your face, the smell, the scent of it and to be on the top of the waves without a care in the world. They all sat talking and sharing the food the ladies had brought with them.

It was fun, it was so different to be in the company of young people so alive so free spirited, it had been a long, long time since she had enjoyed herself like this.

As Anna walked with them toward the sea, the closer she came she felt like she was forgetting something- leaving something behind.

"I can't," Anna said a little too loudly. She stopped in her tracks and was aware they had all stopped too.

"Hey, it's okay, we can all meet up again soon. We can find you, where are you staying?" One of the ladies named Joanne asked.

"At the temple." Anna replied and then suddenly a smile that went so deep shone upon her face.

"Thank you, thank you all for such a fun day, but I know in my heart I belong at the temple."

Anna almost skipped back to the temple, "Why did she suddenly feel so free," she wondered.

CHAPTER 4

He's Back

A shaft of light poured into the windowless room waking Anna and almost blinding her. It was around three in the morning and the whole room was filled with light. As she lifted her head from her pillow, she heard a clear strong, all knowing, powerful voice speak into her heart."

"You love Me!"

Anna arose from the bed and with the Joy of the Lord flooding her entire being she jumped for Joy and danced as if with Him and smiled and rejoiced in His Glorious Presence around her tiny room.

Tears of love saturated her night dress as she poured out her love for Him over and over, intoxicated in His Presence.

She lifted her pillow as if holding Him and cried out to Him.

"I love You; I love You; I love You!"

The words gushed out before she realized what she was saying.

"My beloved is mine and I am His." Her smile was beaming, and she felt within herself, like He was smiling through her. His Presence too beautiful to describe.

In her boldness and great Joy, she exclaimed "Should You not have kissed me first?"

And then as if burning through her came His reply.

"I did."

Anna laughed as He caused her to remember all that time ago when they first met on the tiled floor of the temple, when the wind had blown against her veil, and how it had felt she recalled "Just like a kiss on her lips." Anna blushed.

"I've missed You, don't leave me again, O how I've missed You!"

Everything she had been through was worth this moment with Him. And as she thought it, another burst of Joy flooded her senses.

"Were You testing me, did you doubt my love, what if I wanted to test You?"

"I will prove My love!"

No sooner were the words imparted in her heart than a chill and sadness indescribable swept through her, and a thought occurred to her, if this were the test, He would put her through, what was the test The Living God Himself would go through?

"My Beloved," Anna sung out, lightning the mood once again, "Come let us walk together, I'm too excited to sleep and I don't want to waste a moment."

Suddenly the light in the room was gone and for the briefest moment Anna was afraid He had left, until deep in her spirit that was now flooded with His, she heard Him say.

"Fear not, I AM with you!"

She laughed as she felt the slightest touch of His hand in hers and He led her out into the new day.

Anna talked nonstop along the path with her Lord. It never occurred to her that someone may have seen her talking to herself. She was far too excited, and nothing could dampen her mood. He whom her heart loved was with her. He had taken hold of her hand in His righteous right hand, and she smiled, and He smiled within her.

She skipped and twirled and felt free and young and beautiful and loved - O so loved.

She bent down to pick Him a flower. As she went to speak, her mouth was filled with a language she had never spoken. It was unearthly and beautiful and instinctively she knew it was His heavenly language, and that she was speaking directly to His heart, words unutterable. Tears flowed down her cheeks at the precious gift He had bestowed on her.

Anna kept on speaking- praying all day, walking and stopping to say to Him with laughter in her voice.

"I hope in all that I have spoken I have told You - how much I love You."

Anna's body reacted to the Power of His Love by almost doubling over under the weight. It was not unpleasant, nor was it painful. But unlike anything she had ever experienced. And though it only lasted a brief moment, she knew The Holy God who had created the heavens and the earth was responding to her love for Him.

CHAPTER 5

The Promise

Anna spoke the language of God more now than the language she was raised with. She sang in the new spiritual language and even under her breath she heard herself uttering the words foreign to her and yet more comfortable and natural.

Within weeks of praying like this at all hours of the day and night- Anna felt herself begin to strengthen. Doubts slowly began to fade away. She was surrendering to a new level of His call upon her life. He wanted everything, to have her completely to Himself for His purpose and His plan, which He slowly began to reveal.

As she woke one morning, a scripture filled her heart and mind and all through the morning it lingered.

"Because He loves Me," says the Lord, "I will rescue him, I will protect him, for he acknowledges My Name. He will call upon Me, and I will answer him, I will be with him in trouble, I will deliver him and honour him. With long life I will satisfy him and show him My Salvation."

Anna went about her day kneeling on the secret cushion on the hard tiles praying and singing and talking to her beloved Lord. She felt stirred in her spirit to take a walk around the temple and made her way to the outer courts.

She watched people of all ages milling around, as if they were waiting for something. Then when she looked toward the column in the opposite direction, she saw what they were waiting on. A rabbi was walking towards them with his disciples right behind him.

There was much excitement in the atmosphere and Anna grew curious to see and hear this rabbi that was so close now that she could hear him. The crowds of people began to merge tightly together and then sat on the ground to listen.

Someone noticed her still standing and called for her to sit - so in obedience Anna sat.

And for the first time since her father and her husband had taught her, she was now in the presence of a real teacher being taught The Word of God.

The rabbi spoke so clearly and was as rivers of Living Water flowing right from him to fill her. Anna drank so deeply and then something so unexpected happened that it made her laugh. All eyes turned to her, and she felt the skin on her face turn red and hot, and quickly got up and scurried away.

The rabbi was teaching on the Psalms and when he got to the words "Because he loves me," Says the lord, "I will rescue him. I will protect him, for he acknowledges My Name"

"That's the same scripture from this morning," Anna thought to herself, amused by the coincidence.

"He will call upon Me, and I will answer him; I will be with him in trouble, I will deliver him and honour him. With long life I will satisfy him and show him My salvation."

Every word was like it was being spoken just to her but of course that could not be. Anna walked back into the temple and was on her way to her room when the woman of great age who had shown her the room and placed a bowl of food before her sprang up out of nowhere and reached for her arm.

For what seemed like an awfully long time she just stood eyes fixed on her face. Anna was unsure whether she should say something when the woman spoke so softly Anna had to strain to hear.

"Because he loves Me," Says the Lord, I will rescue him,"

Anna fell to her knees- the aged woman continued on, still clinging to her arm.

"I will protect him, for he acknowledges My Name. He will call upon Me and I will answer him. I will be with him in trouble. I will deliver him and honour him. With long life will I satisfy him,"

"And show him- My Salvation."

Anna opened her eyes, and she was all alone, tears running down her face.

She began rocking and the words were building up inside of her needing to be released - spoken out.

"Because he loves me,"

Anna started to cry heavy tears, her heart and soul connecting to The Word of GOD- The Word of Life.

"Because he loves Me," says the Lord.

"I will rescue him; I will protect him."

And then like a light going on, Anna began again.

"Because she loves Me, Says the Lord"- A great current swept through her body.

"I will rescue her," between each line she groaned from the depths of her being.

"I will protect her, for she acknowledges My Name

She will call upon Me, and I will answer her,

I will be with her in trouble I will deliver her and honour her,

with long life I will satisfy her, and show her..."

Anna's mouth gaped open as the enormity of what she was speaking impacted, with all her amazing experiences of the Living God, this one was like crackers going off inside her.

"And show her," She repeated, grinning from ear to ear barely able to contain what she knew without a doubt that He was speaking personally to her.

"And show her- My Salvation."

Anna rolled over onto her back threw her legs up in the air and giggled like a child.

"He loves me!"

That was the first of many, many times The Living God tried to impart His Truth to Anna. She received His Word always with childlike enthusiasm, aching to hear how much He loved her.

He was so patient with her as the years rolled on, and their relationship grew. She clung to Him and laughed with Him and told Him stories and always reminded Him, how loved He was. Never did a day go past without her pouring out her heart to Him.

At one time she tried to join up with the other people in the outer courts of the temple to hear the rabbi preach, but the rabbi remembered her, and not well. In front of everyone he told her as she sat to listen with the others, "That here was a young lady quite spirited, and yet not destined to serve in the temple."

She ran from him, by the time she got back to the room she was angry-really angry and she voiced it all with the Lord.

"How dare he publicly humiliate me in such a way, what would he know?"

On and on she went till eventually the Holy Spirit of God withdrew. When she finally calmed down, and that took a long time, as she never got over things like that quickly, He spoke to her, and it cut her to the quick.

"I did not ask you to learn from another!"

Anna was still in a place that she longed to get her point across, to argue her case, and she nearly did, but then suddenly the reminder of the months without Him came into her heart.

"Well," she softened "Teach me, show me Your ways - help me to understand the words You gift to me."

And with much love and tenderness He did.

As she slept, her heart was awake, and He fed her His Word. In the morning she would rise up singing. The more she prayed in the Spirit the deeper the revelation, the more she understood, the more she hungered for Him."

He playfully teased her when He showed her in a dream, "It is the Glory of God to conceal a matter, and the Glory of a king to search it out." "How can I search?" She woke up saying.

"They won't let me read Your Holy Scriptures and I wouldn't understand them anyway."

Anna paced that day, praying in the Spirit whilst her mind was active as to how she could search out the scriptures.

A brilliant plan came to mind, as she thought it through, she wondered if He would be mad or merely amused. She could dress as a man and sneak in and hear the Word of God. Perhaps she could sneak a scroll back to her room just for a night.

Hours ticked by, deciding the best way to acquire a man's robe. It even crossed her mind she could somehow borrow her father's, whom she hadn't seen now for years.

And then as if He had heard her every thought the words He'd once said echoed through the chambers of her heart.

"I did not ask you to learn from another!"

This time there was no mistaking it. He was angry...

Or so she thought.

CHAPTER 6

The Fragrance of Him

Late that evening, whilst sitting on the cushion on the tiles, not praying, not talking, not singing, merely meditating on the powerful Word He had brought to her in three confirming ways.

"With long life I will satisfy her and show her My Salvation."

Though she hungered to understand, it was like a veil was in front of her eyes. "I will deliver her and honour her; how can it be? How can I, a woman, understand? How can I be honoured? How can I know things too wonderful for me to know?

"How can You show me Your Salvation?"

Deep in thought, a gentle breeze blew against her skin, she smiled so sure it was Him. And then a beautiful fragrance filled the air all around her. It was roses and lilies it was the scent of Love she was sure of it. A single tear rolled down her cheek and something made her open her eyes and right there beside her was the aged woman kneeling on the hard tiles, her arms lifted in praise. In that moment her face was radiant she looked young and beautiful but there was no mistaking it -it was her... The mysterious woman she had met briefly twice.

Anna breathed in deeply and became intoxicated in His Love. "The scent," She began to say, "Can you smell the scent?"

"It is the Lord!" Her voice was pure.

For a long time, they both remained in silence. Anna watched the woman in perfect stillness. Her face shone, her eyes were closed, it was then she noticed the brightness of her robe - whiter than white.

"Who is this woman?" As soon as the thought came into her mind, the woman opened her eyes and turned to her.

"Anna"

"You know me. you know my name?" Anna stammered in awe.

"Anna, He wants you to know Him"

Before a word even formed on Anna's lips to reply, the woman spoke, with such power and such knowing, that Anna lifted her shawl higher about her as if to hide from her all-knowing, all-seeing eyes.

"Don't be afraid, the Lord Your God is with you, He is mighty to save, He will take great delight in you. He will quiet you with His love, He will rejoice over you with singing."

"I love Him" Anna said shyly "He is my friend!"

"Holy, Holy, Holy is the Lord God Almighty who was, and is, and is to come."

Every word was Spirit breathed; every word took Anna up higher as she herself humbled herself lower.

"You are Worthy, our Lord and God, to receive Glory and Honour and Power, for You created all things, and by Your will they were created and have their being."

"You are worthy to take the scroll and to open its seal, because You were slain, and with Your blood, You purchased men for God." Anna groaned a deep guttural sound.

The woman continued, and as she spoke, revelation was poured in. Anna's spirit was receiving, what her mind could not - yet.

"From every tribe and language and people and nation, You made them to be a Kingdom and Priests to serve our God and they will reign on the earth."

The woman reached out her hand and hovered it just over Anna, then ever so gently touched her and the touch was like lightening. "Worthy is the Lamb, who was slain, to receive power and wealth and wisdom and strength and honour and glory and praise."

"He wants you to know Him!"

Anna lost a day and a half. She woke on the floor. Someone had thrown a rug over her. She had no memory of what had happened with those missing hours. But she was not the same.

Anna the girl was gone now, Anna the woman was emerging submitted, full of the fear of the Lord. Her love for Him overflowed her heart, but it ran deeper now. His Words flowed from her lips, Words she had never even learned.

More and more she would find herself awakening before the dawn to walk her treasured walk to the Mount of Olives and on the way, she would speak out His Word, that He had placed within her.

"The Sovereign Lord has given Me an instructed tongue, to know The Word that sustains the weary. He wakens me morning by morning, wakens my ear to listen like one being taught. The Sovereign Lord has opened My ears and I have not been rebellious, I have not drawn back".

"I offered My back to those who beat Me, My cheeks to those who pulled out My beard; I did not hide My face from mocking and spitting. Because the Sovereign Lord helps Me, I will not be disgraced. Therefore, I have set My face like flint, and I know I will not be put to shame."

"This is You! This is You! You said to me all those years ago, that You would prove Your love." Anna was stunned, she knew He was coming to the earth that He had created, scriptures new and old were filling her thoughts and then it really hit, and she fell to the ground. "You were slain, No!" She cried out "No it can't be!" and then in deep anguish she cried out to her Father, "This cannot be Your will, Father this cannot be Your will!"

His still soft voice broke through "For God - your God, so loved the world, that He gave His Only Son, that whosoever believes in Him shall not perish but have everlasting life." His every Word was love poured out, and she knew with all her heart this was the very will of Him, the very heart of Him.

Anna wiped the tears from her eyes and with a determination to please Him, even though her heart was aching beyond anything she experienced she asked.

"In the days ahead help me to do what You require of me, strengthen me, for You have not shown me so much without a reason, a purpose - help me Lord to fulfil, what You ask of me."

CHAPTER 7

Surrender

Late in the evening in the following week, the woman suddenly appeared as she did the last time kneeling on the tiles by Anna. That same fragrance was present, and the peace that surpassed all understanding seemed to flow with her. Anna opened her eyes to see the woman smiling at her, a gentle look on her face as if she were searching every little thing about her.

This time Anna had no intention of allowing the woman to leave without knowing something about her. Somehow, she knew she would ask questions of her this time.

Anna turned her face away for a brief moment resting her eyes on the burning lamp, she needed to show respect to this woman, but she wanted to know so much about her, "Help me Lord to ask the right questions," Anna prayed silently.

The woman's smile changed to a grin and even in the atmosphere it could be felt that subtle change, without even seeing her face.

Anna felt drawn to look at the woman's face again and as she did the warmth and purity were there but there was much joy all over her face, pouring through her eyes.

"I was like you, young and so in love." The woman took a moment to reflect and carefully choose her words.

"He changed me, slowly over time."

Anna's face dropped like she had heard unwelcome news.

"He has molded me and taught me, and it has been a fully yielded life." Her voice was gentle and soothing.

"My joy is His, my tears and pain are His, my life is His. I live for Him. He has been to me Father, friend, family. There has been a price to pay for what He has shown me and what He has called me to do. I sup alone, and I walk alone. He has called me to a life of prayer. To pray in His will, His wonderful plan."

"It is a life most blessed and most alone. He has revealed Himself to me in the most powerful ways. He has broken me and watched everything taken away from me. He has asked of me things I yet don't understand, and leaves me that I might always be in a place where I hunger for Him."

"I hear His voice and know His Presence. I have never married or held the hand of a man. I was the orphan baby raised for His purpose, right here at the temple. And I am so loved of Him, that when it came time for me to leave the temple as a young woman to begin a life, every door closed before me that I might stay with Him."

"Anna the life He has called you to is connected in prayer to the life He has called me to."

Anna stared at the old woman in front of her.

"Are you still so in love with Him?" Anna's heart was being revealed, she was so afraid of losing this place she had found with Him, that she questioned the thing that concerned her most.

"I told you, I was young and so in love, now I am old, much older and He is - to me all that He has revealed to me. He is God, Holy God. My love for Him now is as the Holy God of Israel." Though she spoke gently it was with much emphasis.

Anna's tears could not be held back, "Then I can't, I can't!"

Anna arose and ran from the temple to the Mount of Olives. The woman's words burning within her as she raced away.

"What you have for Him is romantic love, know Him Anna - Know Him!"

The moon was shining brightly as Anna raced along her familiar path to the mount of Olives, for the first time in a long time, she really felt alone.

She questioned herself as she ran. Did she really love Him wrongly? He had drawn her, and wooed her, He was so easy to fall in love with. Was it just too romantic the way she left flowers for Him daily and sang Him personal love songs, but surely, they were Holy Spirit led?

Tears were flowing and her mind was whirling, "But You are my everything!" She cried. "Not just the Holy God of Israel, But the God of all creation, the friend who listens, the Father who just loves me, You are my love. All my love belongs with You. You are my lover in my arms as I dance when no one sees. I am passionately in love with You. Every fibre of my being screams out for more of You, and I don't even know what the more is! And though I have never seen You I love You, and still I have not seen You. I believe in You."

"I am a rose of Sharon- a Lily of the valley." Anna felt like she had been poured out like a drink offering, like there was nothing more inside of her to give, the empty vessel.

The sound of thunder was heard over head, what had once been a clear night was now electrified as lightning blazed across the skies, the moon hidden by dark clouds. A mighty wind was roaring through the leaves in the trees, all the branches were swaying.

Then as quickly and as strangely as it began, it stopped, and the moon reappeared. Anna went to take a step and there at her feet lay a single Lily. She bent down to pick up the flower and heard the sound of thunder, so powerful, so deafening and then came The Voice of The Lord.

"Like a Lily among thorns is my darling among the maidens."

Anna scooped up the Lily in her hands and stood under the moon light overwhelmed in awe and fear and love. Then lifting the Lily high in the air, she took a step and then another and began to dance. A gently breeze blew across her face and Anna took her queue and blew Him a kiss.

"You love my love, don't You?" She whispered smiling, "Well guess what, I love Yours."

CHAPTER 8

Learning to Pray

When Anna came back to the temple it was late, it was dark, but she knew the woman would still be awake somewhere in the temple praying and if she had to search all night, all morning she would until she found her.

Anna had no intention of letting her remarks just be forgotten, they had stung, and she would somehow let her know just how wrong she was.

The Temple was huge but there were many places a woman could not enter. Anna searched the obvious places first, preparing what she would say with every new room she ventured.

After hours of looking, she walked outside and to the outer courts and it was there she found her, pacing, praying.

Sometimes the words came out in Hebrew and others were in the spirit. Her eyes were lifted to the heavens as the words poured forth from her lips. Anna listened as the fragrance of the Lord wrapped around her. The woman was so deep in prayer she had not yet noticed Anna approach.

"A voice of one calling in the desert - prepare the way for The Lord-make straight in the wilderness a highway for our God. A voice of one calling, calling in the desert."

Then the most powerful prayer Anna had ever heard uttered prayed in the spiritual language with force and power, flowed from this woman's lips. The force of the prayer was causing the woman to come down to a crouching position like she was giving birth and on and on she prayed.

This was prayer with intensity and purpose, and even though not familiar, Anna knew she would learn to pray in power, like this. Her own thoughts in wanting to prove herself, her point no longer seemed important, she had to bury her pride and learn from this woman.

Suddenly the woman through pure exhaustion, cried out leaning forward, no longer words nor spiritual tongues, this was groaning, but not of this earth. This was other worldly. The woman was truly praying through a prayer for the living God. Perspiration was beading on her face; her eyes were no longer seeing anything before her. Though they were fixed on something or Anna thought "Someone."

Anna reached out her hand and took hold of the woman's hand. Immediately it was crushed in her tightly clenched hand. The powerful anointing knocked Anna off her feet as she was so unprepared for the transference through their hands. Anna pulled herself up to the squatting position and the two of them hand in hand, allowed the Holy Spirit to work through them.

After hours of praying in such a manner, the intensity stilled, and their hands came apart. This beautiful, aged woman now lay where she had prayed, and an hour passed before she spoke.

"Thank you, thank you." She turned her face and smiled at Anna.

"I feel like I just gave birth." she laughed, and it was totally unexpected. It made Anna bubble over with laughter.

"You passed your test by the way" she said raising herself up on her elbow.

"What test?" Anna asked.

"Except one thing, small but very important" she said grinning at Anna.
"What test, what one thing, what are you talking about?"

"Anna, I am in love with my God, head over heels, mind blowing mountains, can't live without Him, could you not discern? I wear His very fragrance, I walk in His love, my cup overflows with His Joy. Did you really think I could live here in the temple all these years and not be "so in love with Him?"

"But you said."

"I wanted to know, not Him, I alone wanted to know if you would really love Him passionately as He loves you!"

"Why, why would you do that?"

"Because He has chosen you," the woman took a deep breath.

"To pray Him to the very earth He created."

Anna's eyes were wide open staring into the woman's face.

"Nothing happens without prayer, He needs us Anna, He needs us"

Anna shook her head in confusion, this was all too much. "Are you sure, me, He wants me - to pray Him to - O this is too much!"

"But why did you criticise me by saying my love for Him is romantic love, that He just wanted me to know Him?"

"I wanted to push you to see how deep your love for Him is. Others may know Him, line upon line, But God knew when He chose you for this task, He knew your heart, you love Him as he created you to love Him and Him alone. But I didn't know, and I am jealous over Him, tenderly will I care for Him.

"You said He needs us; do we pray for Him together?"

"He has chosen you, blessed are you, that no one knows and yet your relationship is most intimate, you will see His salvation- He has promised you!"

"I will see Him" Anna said out loud trying to take it in, my eyes will behold the Glory of God" The woman just smiled the most serene smile, like she understood far more than she had ever said.

"What's your name?" Anna asked.

Suddenly the older woman began to beam with the most beautiful smile.

"He has called me Hephzibah, so you may call me Hephzibah." She grinned each time she mentioned her name.

"Do you know what it means?"

"My delight is in her" She threw her head back and laughed. "He delights in me, Anna and I in Him." She lifted her hands to the heavens grinning as a woman in love and cried out "I delight greatly in the Lord; my soul rejoices greatly in my God."

"It's like were both in love with the same......," Anna's words were left hanging in the air, because both knew that though He is God- to them He was their love, He was the man in their life, it made no sense with the mind. Only with the heart. Anna reached for her cheeks knowing she was blushing. The two women reached for each other's hands, one well into her nineties, or perhaps even older still, the other in her late twenties and gently squeezed the others hand in silent understanding.

Hephzibah arose straightened out her robe and kissed Anna on the cheek. "Goodnight beloved of the Lord."

"You haven't told me what you are to pray," Anna said yawning.

"Another day."

Anna glanced up at the stars then turned her attention back and the woman was gone.

CHAPTER 9

The Call

Weeks turned to months before the two women met again even though Anna looked for her. She went over and over the last encounter they'd had together every small detail and was still over awed by the news that it was she who would pray her Beloved to the earth.

Strangely instead of praying more in the spirit, Anna had ceased to pray at all. She was afraid of the prayer she might pray. There was so much she didn't understand. She talked to Him and asked Him questions, but silence was His reply.

The rains were falling heavily, and she could not get out for her much-needed walk. The Kidron brook would be flowing and how she longed to be crossing it and on her way to her most favorite place of all- high up on a mountain so high it was like touching heaven. Once when a cloud appeared and enveloped her, she almost imagined hearing a voice coming from the cloud, she would lay on her back and try to see an opening into heaven.

Hephzibah was as usual silent as she made her way to the tiles beside Anna, she never uttered a word for a long time. Anna on the other hand was so excited to see her, that she strained like holding back the tide to not say something.

"Anna," The woman reached over to touch her hand and kissed it.

"Anna, please listen to me as I speak what I must, ask no questions of me." Tears sat brimming in her eyes, her face was radiant -something was different.

Anna in turn kissed her hand and went to wipe her tears but she pulled away.

"Anna, I have great news, and as happy as I am by the news, I know it will cause you pain and confusion."

Anna sat on her bottom and faced her, how unfair not to be allowed to ask a question because she had many.

"Anna that which the Lord had entrusted to me, the call on my life has been fulfilled, on that very last night with you. I was to pray for the one who would prepare the way for the Lord. He made it known to me I would not live to see him, but that I would know when it was time to come home."

Anna started to cry.

"My work is done, yours is just beginning- He loves you, He says to you, "Don't be afraid."

"Just one question, please just one." Anna begged.

"Permit me to say what I must and then you may."

Anna nodded and sobbed. Her only friend was being taken away, she was just getting to know her, and wanted to share more time with her.

"Don't be afraid to pray."

Anna stared hard at the tiles, He was talking to her, though it was the woman's voice it was Him, and all her fears just melted away, He knew her, better than she knew herself.

"You will have a long life and you will see Him, in the years to come, cling to Him, no matter how hard life may become. He will never leave you. Will you do this for Him?"

Anna nodded and smiled as she saw the smile on Hephzibah's face.

"When I go don't grieve as someone who has no hope, He has promised us Life Eternal, I am not sick, He is merely calling me home, be pleased for me!"

Anna mouthed the words "I'll try."

"So, what is your one question?"

Anna grinned as she thought about the things that puzzled her most about this extraordinary woman. She thought about the clothes she wore that were whiter than white, and the way she disappeared and appeared so abruptly. The way she knew things, that only the Lord knew. There were so many things about her.

"I want to know how I too, can wear the very fragrance of His Love?" Anna whispered. And as the words were spoken all around them was filled with the scent of Lilies and Roses.

"He knew - He knew you would ask for this, and He leaves His fragrance with you. He is well pleased with you. Love Him forever more deeply without question, with all of your heart, your soul, your mind, all that is within you- Love Him. Prophesy Him to the earth for that is who you are - His prophetess."

Anna turned her head and watched her walk away, knowing it was the last time on this earth she would see her, and yet she was filled with Joy - Joy unspeakable.

CHAPTER 10

Sitting at His Feet

Month after month, and year after year, Anna grew in her love for her Lord. She no longer questioned her own hunger for Him or the life she lived. It was all normal to her, she ate Him and drank and prayed Him and sang to Him and every moment was consumed in Him. She would run along her path to the Mount of Olives and know He was with her- His presence so very real. There was something about this place that went beyond her understanding, it went beyond reason, and though she loved the temple over the years it became clear that it was in the Mount of Olives that she felt closest with Him.

The more she understood in her heart, soul, mind and emotions that she was really praying Him to this place. Not just to the earth, but to this place, that we are His people, His peculiar treasure, and that it was here that His feet would walk, Jerusalem His Holy city, the place He loved above all others.

But something began to happen that she could not pull away from. It was taking place deep in her spirit and she never understood and there was no one to ask. It began in her fiftieth year, the week before Passover she would weep at the mention of His Name. She would go and listen to the rabbi's just to hear His every Word spoken out in the temple courts and then each evening she went out to spend the night on the Hill called the Mount of Olives.

She would pray and sing the Psalms to Him, rejoicing before Him in His inhabited world. Often, she would turn her head expecting to see Him as His presence was so strong. It was like He was singing with her, leading her by the hand walking through the trees, looking up at the stars that displayed the Glory of God Himself.

On the first day of unleavened bread preparations were being made to celebrate the Passover. As evening approached all over Jerusalem, the Jewish people were celebrating the feast of unleavened bread because it was on this very day that God brought our divisions out of Egypt. "Celebrate this day," He said, "as a lasting ordinance for the generations to come."

"Tell the whole community of Israel that on the tenth day of this Month each man is to take a lamb for his family, one for each household. If any household is too small for a whole lamb, they must share one with their nearest neighbor, having taken into account the number of people there are. You are to determine the amount of lamb needed in accordance with what each person will eat."

"The animals you choose must be year old males without defect, and you may take them from the sheep or the goats. Take care of them until the fourteenth day of the month, when all the people of the community of Israel must slaughter them at twilight. Then they are to take some of the blood and put it on the sides and tops of the doorframes of the houses where they eat the lambs."

"That same night they are to eat the meat roasted over the fire, along with bitter herbs, and bread made without yeast. Do not eat the meat raw or cooked in water, but roast it over the fire- head, legs and inner parts. Do not leave any of it till morning, if some is left till morning, you must burn it."

"This is how you are to eat it with your cloak tucked into your belt, your sandals on your feet and your staff in your hand. Eat it in haste. It is the Lord's Passover."

"On that same night I will pass through Egypt and strike down every firstborn - both men and animals, and I will bring judgement on the gods of Egypt. I Am The Lord. The blood will be a sign for you on the houses where you are and when I see the blood, I will Passover you. No destructive plague will touch you when I strike Egypt."

"In the first month eat bread made without yeast, from the evening of the fourteenth day until the evening of the twenty first day. For seven days no yeast is to be found in your houses. And whoever eats anything with yeast in it, must be cut off from the community of Israel, whether he is an alien or native born. Eat nothing made with yeast. Wherever you live, you must eat unleavened bread."

The very words of Moses that her father had taught her as a young girl flooded her mind as she recalled he commanded the elders of Israel, "Go and select the animals for your families and slaughter the Passover lamb. Take a bunch of Hyssop, dip it into the blood in the basin and put some of the blood on the top and on both sides of the doorframe."

"Not one of you shall go out the door of his house until morning. When the Lord goes through the land to strike down the Egyptians, He will see the blood on the top and sides of the doorframe and will Passover that doorway, and He will not permit the destroyer to enter your houses and strike you down."

The wind was blowing through the leaves in the trees. Anna thought it sounded like words, a question being asked. "When your children ask you

What do you mean by this ceremony?" Tell them "It is the Passover sacrifice to the Lord, who passed over the houses of the Israelites in Egypt and spared our homes when He struck down the Egyptians." Anna bowed low and worshipped Him.

And every year the week before Passover, she would spend her days in the temple and her nights on the Mount and every year it intensified and every year she would be led by unseen hand to the garden where she felt like all her strength was gone as she cried out in such agony, and she felt like an olive in an olive press. "Gethsemane, what is it about this place, that my soul is overwhelmed with sorrow to the point of death?"

No one would understand, only Him, that after the Sabbath at dawn, on the first day of the week, Joy unspeakable would fill her soul and everything she had experienced had been invisibly washed away.

And back she would go to her quiet life in the temple kneeling on her secret cushion and dancing under the stars with Him or holding a pillow against her heart and imagining it was Him.

CHAPTER 11

I am the Lord thy Healer

Anna lay on the mattress in her tiny room, she was cold, shivering, all her bones ached. Something was wrong. All her energy was gone as she lay just breathing, listening to the sound of her own heartbeat, too weak to call out. She thirsted but was unable to lift herself from her mattress.

In the windowless room, Anna lost track of time, conscious at times and others, her mind was like a stranger to her. Sounds became something to focus on almost soothing, she began to wonder if someone had entered the room. desperately she tried to lift her head only to pass out.

Waking sometime later, she thought someone was sitting on a seat in her room right by her head.

"I thirst," She breathed. Her tongue and mouth so dry. Did she make a sound at all? she wondered.

She thought she heard her mother's voice; it came from another room. She was being taken care of. Her father was home, he had been gone a long time, but mother never complained, he loved his work in the temple.

Perhaps he would sit by her bed and tell her about the Lord. He often did that when she was sick. He was just so quiet now. The room was constantly dark now as the oil had run out. Everything was confused and then someone took her hand. She did not know who it was until he spoke. She knew his voice even in the dark. It was her father.

"Anna let me wash you in the Word of God"

Tears flowed from her eyes as her father shared with her one his favorite sections in the Word. He knew it all by heart and it just poured out of him.

"Hezekiah sent word to all Israel and Judah and also wrote letters to Ephraim and Manasseh inviting them to come to the temple of The Lord in Jerusalem and celebrate the Passover to the Lord, the God of Israel."

"The king and his officials and the whole assembly in Jerusalem decided to celebrate the Passover in the Second month. They had not been able to celebrate it at the regular time because not enough priests had consecrated themselves and the people had not assembled in Jerusalem."

"The plan seemed right to the king and to the whole assembly. They decided to send a proclamation throughout Israel, from Beersheba to Dan, calling the people to come to Jerusalem and celebrate the Passover to the Lord, The God of Israel. It had not been celebrated in large numbers according to what was written."

"At the Kings command, couriers went throughout Israel and Judah with letters from the king and from his officials, which read:

"People Of Israel, return to the Lord, the God of Abraham, Isaac and Israel, that He may return to you who are left, who have escaped from the hand of the kings of Assyria. Do not be like your fathers and brothers, who were unfaithful to the Lord, the God of their fathers, so that He made them an object of horror, as you see."

"Do not be stiff necked, as your fathers were, submit to the Lord. Come to the Sanctuary, which He has consecrated forever. Serve the Lord your

God, so that His fierce anger will turn away from you. If you return to the Lord, then your brothers and your children will be shown compassion by their captors and will come back to this land, for the Lord your God is gracious and compassionate. He will not turn His face from you if you return to Him."

"The couriers went from town to town in Ephraim and Manasseh, as far as Zebulun, but the people scorned and ridiculed them. Nevertheless, some men of Asher, Manasseh and Zebulun humbled themselves and went to Jerusalem."

"Did you hear that Anna, the men of Asher - the tribe of Asher humbled themselves - this is our tribe. These are our people. It's who we are, humble and obedient - we returned to Him, He is our God." Her father raised his voice with pride and excitement, and then he continued, and Anna lay silently listening.

"A very large crowd of people assembled in Jerusalem to celebrate the Feast of Unleavened Bread, in the second month. They removed the altars in Jerusalem and cleared away the incense altars and threw them into the Kidron Valley."

"They slaughtered the Passover Lamb on the 14th day of the second month. The priests and the Levites were ashamed and consecrated themselves and brought burnt offerings to the temple of the Lord. Then they took up their regular positions as prescribed in the Law of Moses the man of God. The priests sprinkled the blood handed to them by the Levities. Since many in the crowd had not consecrated themselves, the Levities had to kill the Passover lambs for all those who were not ceremonially clean and could not consecrate their lambs to the Lord."

Although most of the many people who came from Ephraim, Manasseh, Issachar and Zebulun had not purified themselves yet, they ate the Passover, contrary to what was written. But Hezekiah prayed for them saying,

Her father stood to his feet and emphasized each word he spoke.

"May the Lord, who is good, pardon everyone who sets his heart on seeking God- the Lord- the God of his fathers, even if he is not clean according to the rules of the sanctuary."

"And the Lord heard Hezekiah and healed the people!"

"Did you hear that Anna, how merciful is our God, that He allowed man to stand in the gap for man and pray for forgiveness. The Lords Passover was not on the first month as He had commanded because the temple needed to be cleaned and purified of all the idols, not all the priests had consecrated themselves, not all the people had purified themselves and yet, He answered Hezekiah's prayer and forgave and healed all the people - they ate the Passover lamb!"

Anna lay in the silence and her mind unlocked the keys her father had shared, she turned her head to see him, and no one was there, just blackness. Her head was pounding she was lightheaded.

"Place the blood on the top and the sides of the door frame, and He will not permit the destroyer to enter your house and strike you down." With closed eyes Anna imagined the door and saw the blood being sprinkled. The colour red on the right and on the left and then in her mind she looked up and saw the blood on the top of the door frame, the wooden door. And then as she stared at it, she saw something - not the door, but the wood, and she saw the blood at the same height, and it was flowing down." And she started to cry.

She imagined in her mind, tasting of the Lord's Passover lamb and hearing Hezekiah words of prayer, and she spoke what she knew to be true, "The Lord heard, and healed the people." Suddenly a light filled the room and her, and a warmth filled every fibre of her being. She sat up clear in mind and thought, healed of all sickness and yet tears still ran down her face and her thirst was stronger than ever. How long, she wondered, have I been here?

She rose from her bed and drank of the water in the room. It was fresh, and her tears continued to flow as she thought of hearing her father and the love he had of The Word of God. He taught her all those treasured things when she was a young girl under his roof. He had been gone such a long time now, that to hear his voice again in the midst of her darkest days brought back all those memories.

Anna walked outside the temple and into daylight unaware that people were looking at her. She walked and walked to her favorite place and sat on the grass and took off her sandals. She felt alive and restored. She did not notice how white her robes were like they were shining. All that truly held her attention was what she saw, like her eyes were still focused on the Blood and the wood, she looked up to the heavens and cried out, "I saw Your cross."

CHAPTER 12

Jesus is Born

Anna could think of nothing but Him. She saw the signs in the night sky. She knew deep in her spirit, He had come. He had been born. Word was travelling fast, shepherds that had been living out in the fields, keeping watch over their flocks spoke of it. How an angel of the Lord had appeared to them, and the Glory of the Lord shone all around them. They were terrified, But the angel had said to them, "Do not be afraid, I bring you good news of great Joy that will be for all the people. Today in the town of David a Savior has been born to you, He is Christ the Lord."

They had said how, "This would be a sign to you, you will find a baby wrapped in cloths and lying in a manger." Suddenly a great company of the heavenly host appeared with the angel, praising God and saying,

"Glory to God in the Highest and on the earth Peace to men on whom His favour rests." Anna heard that when the Angels had left them and gone into heaven the shepherds said to one another, "Let's Go to Bethlehem and see this thing that has happened, which the Lord has told us about."

They hurried off and found Mary and Joseph, and the baby, who was lying in the manger. When they had seen Him, they spread the Word about this child and all who heard it were amazed at what the shepherds had said to them.

Anna could not contain her excitement, and with each moment it bubbled up inside of her. Great Joy was filling her every waking moment and sometimes tears trickled down her cheeks and her smile never left her face.

She knew the Jewish custom, that it would be within forty days she would see Him, the one her heart loved. On the fortieth day after His birth, He would be brought into the very temple that had become her home - The Father's house of prayer. And He would be presented to the Lord.

Anna couldn't sit still on her cushion; her thoughts were overflowing with thoughts of Him. After all these years in the temple praying, drawing Him, prophesying since her twenties she would see Him. The years had crept up on her and at eighty-four, the answer to her prayer was here. The day of the Lord had come.

Over the years the Lord had taught Anna patience but this day and the days following, her yearning to see Him became intolerable, the waiting was harder than all the years of loneliness, and everything she had suffered in the silence within the temple and within her heart.

She walked to the Mount of Olives and noticed all the Lilies growing wildly along the lower paths leading to the green pastures. Nothing would ever be the same again, not for her nor for anyone because, He was here.

He was here to make "All things New," and try as she might she could not quite imagine Him the creator of all things, the Majesty of Heaven in all the fullness of the Godhead bodily as a baby - helpless and totally dependent on mankind the very ones He came to save.

"Father, You are Faithful and True, You promised Your people their Redeemer, their Saviour." Anna lifted her eyes to heaven and Holy Words poured forth out of her mouth and she knew once again He was using her to prophesy.

"Nevertheless, there will be no more gloom, for those who were in distress. In the past he humbled the land of Zebulun and the Naphtali, but in the future, He will honour Galilee of the Gentiles, by the way of the sea, along the Jordan."

"The people walking in darkness have seen a great light, on those living in the land of the shadow of death- a light has dawned. You have enlarged the nation and increased their joy; they rejoice before You as people rejoice at the harvest as men rejoice when dividing the plunder. For as in the day of Midian's defeat You have shattered- the yoke that burdens them, the bar across their shoulders, the rod of their oppressor. Every Warriors boot used in battle and every garment rolled in blood will be destined for burning, will be fuel for the fire."

"For to us a child is born - to us a Son is given, and the government will be on His shoulders. And He will be called Wonderful Counselor, Mighty God, Everlasting Father, Prince of Peace. Of the increase of His government and Peace there will be no end.

"He will reign on David's throne and over His Kingdom establishing and upholding it with Justice and Righteousness from that time on and forever. The Zeal of the Lord Almighty will accomplish this!"

CHAPTER 13

My Covenant

Anna pondered in her heart what would be taking place soon with Jesus, she could vividly recall her father and her late husband talking about The Covenant God Himself had made with Abram.

When Abram was ninety-nine years old, The Lord appeared to him, and said, "I Am God Almighty, walk before Me and be blameless. I will confirm my covenant between Me and you and will greatly increase your numbers."

Abram fell face down, and God said to him, "As for Me, this is My Covenant with you. You will be the father of many nations. No longer will you be called Abram, your name will be Abraham, for I have made you a father of many nations. I will make you very fruitful. I will make nations of you, and Kings will come from you. I will establish My Covenant as an Everlasting Covenant, between Me and you and your descendants after you for the generations to come, to be Your God, and the God of your descendants after you. The whole land of Canaan, where you are now an alien, I will give you an Everlasting possession to you and your descendants after you, and I will be their God."

Then God said to Abraham, "As for you, you must keep My Covenant, you and your descendants after you for the generations to come. This is My Covenant with you and your descendants after you, the Covenant you are to keep. Every male among you shall be circumcised."

"You are to undergo circumcision, and it will be the sign of the Covenant between Me and you. For the generations to come every male among you who is eight days old must be circumcised, including those born in your household or bought with money from a foreigner- those who are not your offspring. Whether born in your household or bought with money they must be circumcised."

"My Covenant in your flesh is to be an Everlasting Covenant. Any uncircumcised male, who has not been circumcised, in the flesh, will be cut off from his people, he has broken My Covenant."

Anna knelt on the tiles as the words of the past flooded the present, she just closed her eyes and could imagine she could hear them, both of them so strong in faith, faithful and obedient to the Word of God.

Her Husband's voice echoing in her ears, as tears of remembrance of days so long ago filled her thoughts.

The Lord said to Moses, "Say to the Israelites, a woman who becomes pregnant and gives birth to a son will be ceremonially unclean for seven days, just as she is unclean during her monthly period. On the eighth day the boy is to be circumcised. Then the woman must wait thirty-three days to be purified from her bleeding. She must not touch anything sacred or go to the sanctuary until the days of her purification are over." Anna wiped the tears away and opened her eyes.

On the eighth day, when it was time to circumcise Him, He was named Jesus, the name the angel had given Him before He had been conceived.

When the time of their purification according to the Law of Moses, had been completed, Joseph and Mary took Him to Jerusalem to present Him to the Lord, as it is written in the Law of the Lord. "Every first-born male is to be consecrated to the Lord" and to offer a sacrifice in keeping with what is said in the Law of the Lord; "a pair of doves or two young pigeons."

There was a man in Jerusalem called Simeon, who was righteous and devout. Anna had spoken to him briefly over the years. He was waiting for the consolation of Israel and the Holy Spirit was upon him. It had been revealed to him that he would not die before he had seen the Lord's Christ.

Anna watched as Simeon moved by the Spirit went into the temple courts. He waited expectantly in silent prayer, an old man even older than Anna herself, yet his face shone with such love. No one would know except the living God the hours this Holy man spent in prayer and his purpose, his wonderful purpose.

His skin was wrinkled and bronzed by the sun, nothing about him would reveal the mighty call on his life. He looked old and ordinary, but Anna knew that this man, quiet and reserved, knew Him, in a way not many would ever come to know.

When the parents bought in the child Jesus to do for Him what the custom of the Law required, Simeon took Him in his arms lifted Him high and praised God saying;

"Now You are releasing Your servant Lord, in Peace according to Your Word, because my eyes have seen Your Salvation - the One You prepared before the face of all the people - a Light for revelation to the Gentiles, and for Glory for Your people Israel." He drew the child close to him and kissed Him repeatedly on the cheeks.

His father and His mother were amazed over what was spoken concerning Him. Then Simeon blessed them and said to Mary His mother;

"This child is destined to cause the falling and rising of many in Israel, and to be a sign that will be spoken against, so that the thoughts of many hearts will be revealed." He seemed to pause for a moment, close to tears and in such awe of what he, Simeon was taking part of. He handed the child Jesus back to His mother and took her hand in his with such tenderness that love poured through as he spoke.

"And a sword will pierce your own soul too."

Anna watched as he withdrew from their presence and knew that his eyes were overflowing with tears. This was the day he had waited for, longed for, prayed and hoped to see with all his heart. His tears were the fulfilment of the promises of his God that he had heard about since he was a little boy.

There was quite a crowd gathered around them now, family, priests, rabbi's and each one took the news of the words spoken and pondered them. Coming up to them at that very moment, Anna gave thanks to God and spoke about the child to all who were looking forward to the redemption of Jerusalem.

Most of them knew who she was. She heard them speaking her name, Anna the Prophetess, the daughter of Phanuel, of the tribe of Asher.

From one to another she walked talking about Him, the One who was their Salvation. This was not her day of tears but of overflowing joy. Her excitement could not be contained. He was here and she wanted above all else for everyone to know and to believe- "That He was God's Son."

Not once did she offer to hold Him in her arms, though she did touch the gentleness of his skin on his hands. Nor did she kiss Him, but she did look into the eyes - His beautiful eyes and in the years to come she wondered what made her react to Him the way she did.

When Joseph and Mary had done everything required by the Law of the Lord, they returned to Galilee to their own town of Nazareth, and in her arms was Jesus and a single Lily that Anna had given to her Lord.

CHAPTER 14

Jesus at twelve

Every year, as is the custom of the Jewish people, the annual attendance at three feasts by all adult males, normally accompanied by their families was commanded in the law. The feast of Passover, Pentecost, and Tabernacles. Distance prevented many from attending all three, but most Jews tried to be at Passover.

And every year Anna was certain in her heart that Jesus' parents went to Jerusalem for the feast of the Passover. But in the crowds of people that filled the area at that time, never once did she imagine seeing Him.

When He was twelve years old, Joseph, Mary and Jesus went up to the feast, according to the custom. After the feast was over, while His parents were returning home, the boy Jesus stayed behind in Jerusalem, but they were unaware of it. Thinking He was in their company they travelled on for a whole day. Then they began looking for Him among their relatives and friends.

When they did not find Him, they went back to Jerusalem to look for Him. After three days they found Him in the Temple courts, sitting among the teachers, listening to them and asking them questions. Everyone who heard Him was amazed at His understanding and His answers.

Anna knew there was so much more in this encounter, so powerful as she looked and listened to Him. For three days it was like He was hidden away, and though He was in open view, speaking to those who listened, it was she who was sure, the Father was revealing something in His being away from those who looked for Him and loved Him.

Anna was not sure at first that He saw her standing at the back of the crowd that was sitting by Him. With her head down not to draw attention to herself she also sat. There were teachers young and old, and they were so interested in what He was saying they never seem to notice her or be bothered by her joining them.

One thing she had decided in her heart, and though it saddened her she believed it to be true, He knew her not! He was a boy - a Son - a Son of the Most High God. But He had come here to this earth that He had created, without any idea of the love she had for Him and the prayers she had prayed for Him. And though He was filled with wisdom and the Grace of God was upon Him, to Him - she was just a very attentive old woman.

Quietly Anna stood to her feet to walk away, when a thought came to mind, so simple and yet so wonderful, she could bring Him a drink of water. She knew He had been there for hours without eating or drinking, perhaps she could take care of Him. She imagined His parents would be back for Him any time soon and He would be returning with them to their home.

Her heart was pounding as she made her way back through the crowd sitting on the ground. She held the cup so carefully so as not to spill even a drop and waited for the right moment when the people were dispersing perhaps for a drink or something to eat themselves. And then like a nervous child, she walked toward Him.

He turned to face her, and the sun was in His face. He lifted His hand to shield His eyes, and she saw the beauty of them. "His eyes are like blazing fire." she thought to herself.

"Woman" He said smiling, "Are you seeking Me?"

Thousands of thoughts invaded her mind at once, "He really doesn't know me", was the one that played over and over. Anna held the cup out to Him not trusting her voice in that moment to come out clear and strong.

Jesus watched her with concern but unable to understand the expression on her face. He took the cup from her hand and drank the water quickly to quench His thirst. He kept watching her, nothing about her was familiar, He had never met her before, and yet there was something - something about her.

"Are You hungry, I can bring something for You," Anna said so quietly she wondered if He had heard her at all. "Will Your parents meet with you soon?"

"I have to be in My Father's house." There was such an urgency almost a desperation, like He was magnetically pulled to this place. Jesus never took His eyes from her face, this old woman, frail and gentle. He watched a silent tear fall down her cheek, and He wanted to pick it up with His fingers and hold it to His lips.

"Do you understand?" He searched her eyes.

Anna looked at the face of the twelve-year-old boy in front of her. With all her heart she wanted to tell Him everything. But if the Father had kept this from Him, He had His reasons, so she would too.

For three days, He was with her in the temple. She gave Him everything she could offer, her small room for Him to lay down and rest, and she slept on the tiles, when she could. Mostly she just prayed and wept and sang to her Father- His Father.,

The small amount of food that she had was all given to Him. She provided for Him with all the love that she felt for her Father, her friend, the One who knew her. It was such a confusing time for Anna, and though it was all her thoughts and prayers had been about for the last seventy years or more, now that He was here, she had to keep it all to herself.

He was a beautiful boy and Anna delighted herself, listening to Him, she never tired of listening to Him as He spoke with rabbis each day. Even then He spoke with such authority- like He knew who He was. She wondered had the revelation of the weight of His purpose for coming to the earth, actually touched Him yet- did He know the price He would pay.

After searching for Him for three days, His parents saw Him, sitting down in the temple courts, with the rabbis listening and asking Questions. His mother said to Him,

"Son, why have You treated us like this? Your father and I have been anxiously searching for You."

And in front of all the learned men, Jesus stood,

"Why were you searching for Me?" He enquired. The look on His face revealed that He meant the words He was saying. He glanced at the two of them, and then at His very surroundings with such a fondness.

"Didn't you know I had to be in My Father's house?"

But they did not understand what He was saying to them, only Anna could feel it in the depths of her heart. He wasn't being disobedient nor brash, He truly was drawn to this place, and He wanted someone to understand.

Anna watched as Jesus and His parents slowly walked away from the temple and from her, returning to their home in Nazareth where they lived. And He was obedient to them. Jesus grew in wisdom and stature and in favour with God and with men.

No one would understand the emptiness she experienced as she climbed the Mount of Olives, knowing with each step they were all taking, it was another step away from Him.

Anna laid on her bed night after night her head on the pillow where His head had laid, and she cried herself to sleep.

"Three days is all You gave me, and now He is gone from my life again. Will I see Him, will He know me, will He ever - remember?"

CHAPTER 15

Baptism

Anna arose early and made her way to the sunshine courtyard and was surprised to find many men sitting on the ground and talking excitedly about a man. Not once in the first while did she hear His Name but she knew, it could only be One. It had to be - Jesus.

The men were animated and so enthralled with their conversation interrupting each other often. Quite a few of them very loud one even jumped up as he was talking.

"It was in the Synagogue everyone was praising Him, it was in Nazareth it was on a Sabbath day, Yom Kippor the day of Atonement. And as was His custom He stood up to read. The scroll of the prophet Isaiah was handed to Him. Unrolling it He found the place where it was written,

"The Spirit of the Lord is on Me, Because He has anointed Me to preach the good news to the poor. He has sent Me to proclaim freedom for the prisoners and recovery of sight for the blind to release the oppressed, to proclaim the year of the Lord's favour."

Then He rolled up the scroll, gave it back to the attendant and sat down. The eyes of everyone in the Synagogue were fastened on Him and He began by saying to them, "Today this scripture is fulfilled in your hearing."

This caused a great commotion with those sitting and each one spoke, but there was one voice though not loud, but it touched Anna's ears and made her smile so deeply.

"I heard from others that every place He went He read that same scripture and confessed that same thing about Himself."

Another voice was raised from a young man perhaps 15 or so full of passion as he shouted above all the others, and it silenced them.

"I have heard from the disciples of John the Baptiser, the son of Zechariah, the one who went into all the country around the Jordan preaching a baptism of repentance for the forgiveness of sins."

Anna's mind wandered back in time to Hephzibah and a silent tear fell from her eyes. "You truly accomplished that which was bestowed upon you, he has come, the one you prayed to the earth."

"A voice of one calling in the desert, prepare the way for the Lord, make straight paths for Him."

More tears fell as she remembered with pure vividness as Hephzibah. had prayed those very words of the prophet Isaiah, and now they had come to pass right before her eyes.

"Every valley shall be filled in, every mountain and hill made low, the crooked roads shall become straight - the rough ways smooth. And all mankind will see God's Salvation." Anna used her prayer shawl to wipe her tears that were falling like rain and splashing down on her feet, as she listened.

"The people were waiting and wondering in their hearts if John might possibly be the Christ. John answered them all, "I baptise you with water, but One more powerful than I will come, the thongs of whose sandals I am not worthy to untie. He will baptise you with the Holy Spirit and with fire. His winnowing fork is in His hand to clear His threshing floor and to gather the wheat into His barn, but He will burn up the chaff with unquenchable fire."

By this time, they were all standing some news cannot be received sitting or reclining. Most were getting quite agitated some appeared to be in shock, but the young man who persistently kept talking above the commotion believed. It was evident to Anna by his face and the passion in which he spoke.

"Then Jesus came from Galilee to the Jordan to be baptised by John, but John tried to deter Him, saying "I need to be baptised by You, and do You come to me."

Jesus replied, "Let it be so now, it is proper for us to do this to fulfill all righteousness," Then John consented.

"John gave this testimony about Him, "I saw the Spirit come down from heaven as a dove and remain on Him. I would not have known, except that the One who sent me to baptise with water, told me. And a voice from heaven said, "This is My Son, whom I Love, with Him I am well pleased"

"The man on whom you see the Spirit come down and remain is He who will baptise with the Holy Spirit. I have seen and I testify that this is the Son of God."

"It was to one of the disciples that was there, who told me, that when John saw Jesus that next day he said, "Behold, the Lamb of God who takes away the sin of the world." That disciple is now following Him!!!" The young man was alive with knowing his face was flooded with such joy and he started to pace and then run around the courtyard yelling and jumping.

"He is here, the Lamb of God, The Messiah - the One we are waiting for- praise God the Holy God of Israel"

The other young men watched stunned at his boldness and enthusiasm, some earnestly disbelieved and tried to keep up with him to silence him, some did not know what to believe, Anna knelt down on the ground and gave thanks with all her heart.

CHAPTER 16

Born Again

It was early- before even the sun had risen. Anna had spent the night in deep prayer, and now she began to pace around the temple, her eyes slowly adjusting to the dimness. She felt refreshed and full of His love as she stepped through the doors and into the freshness of morning. The stars were still shining in the morning skies and the scriptures came to mind and she sang softly as she imagined King David did all those years ago.

"The heavens declare the Glory of God; the skies proclaim the works of His hands. Day after day they pour forth speech, night after night they display knowledge. There is no speech or language where their voice is not heard. Their voice goes out into all the earth, their words to ends of the world."

Anna then heard a strong male voice join in her song and it startled her as she had not noticed anyone in the courtyard.

"In the heavens He has pitched a tent for the sun, which is like a bridegroom coming forth from His pavilion."

Anna walked closer to him and recognized him. "Nicodemus, Israel's great teacher!" Anna smiled. "You have a wonderful voice, please continue." Nicodemus hung his head low and shook it before looking up at her.

"That is the second time I have heard that, in a matter of hours." The emotion in his voice was impossible to miss.

"I went to Him - in the night - alone" He stared up at the sky searching for something.

"Jesus, you went to Jesus," Anna said knowing it could only be Him. After a conversation with Him, one could not be the same, for she knew something had deeply affected Nicodemus.

"Jesus, yes, I came to Him, and I said, "Teacher, we know You are a teacher who has come from God, for no one could perform the miraculous signs You are doing if God were not with Him."

Anna was amazed that this powerful teacher of Israel was talking with her about something so personal and private. There was something about this moment and the weightiness of what Jesus had shared and God Himself had allowed her to be the one he would share it with. Never would this conversation pass from her lips.

"Jesus declared, "I tell you the truth, no one can see the Kingdom of God unless he is born again."

"So, I asked Him, how can a man be born when he is old, surely, he cannot enter a second time into his mother's womb to be born!"

"Jesus answered me, by saying "I tell you the truth, no one can enter the Kingdom of God unless he is born of water and the Spirit."

"He said, "Flesh gives birth to flesh, but the Spirit - gives birth to Spirit." He said you should not be surprised at My saying, "You must be born again. The wind blows wherever it pleases. You hear it's sound, but you cannot tell where it comes from or where it is going. So, it is with everyone born of the Spirit."

"I asked Him, how this could be?" And He replied, "You are Israel's teacher, and you do not understand these things?"

"I tell you the truth, we speak of what we know, and we testify to what we have seen, but still, you people do not accept our testimony."

"I have spoken to you of earthly things, and you do not believe; how then will you believe if I speak of heavenly things? No one has ever gone into heaven except the Son of Man. Just as Moses lifted up the snake in the desert, so the Son of Man must be lifted up, that everyone who believes in Him may have eternal life."

"His next words will never leave my heart, it's almost like, as He spoke, they became a part of me- engraved on my very heart itself." Nicodemus confessed.

"For God so loved the world that He gave His One and Only Son, that whoever believes in Him shall not perish but have Eternal Life'

"For God did not send His Son into the world to condemn the world, but to save the world through Him. Whoever believes in Him is not condemned, but whoever does not believe stands condemned already because he has not believed in the Name of God's One and Only Son."

"This is the verdict: Light has come into the world, but men loved darkness instead of Light - because their deeds were evil. Everyone who does evil hates the Light and will not come into the Light for fear that his deeds will be exposed. But whoever lives by the Truth comes into the Light, so that it may be seen plainly that what he has done has been done through God."

As Nicodemus finished speaking, the morning sun had risen, and they both noticed people were beginning to come into the courtyard. Going against all that she knew Anna slowly reached out her hand from under her prayer shawl - and for the briefest moment - they touched hands.

"Thank you," they both whispered and walked away from each other. Anna pondered the many things she had just learnt in her heart. One thing she knew Nicodemus had to a choice to make - would he choose to believe that the very man who had stood before him, was the Son of God, the Word made flesh?

CHAPTER 17

Living Water

Once again weeks turned to months and so often Anna would hear little fragments of things He was doing and saying to those around Him. Her time was consumed with the love of her heart: the Holy God of Israel, the One she knew. More and more she would wake and find herself praying or talking as if she was part way through conversation. He had promised He would never leave her, and since His Son had come, He Himself had reassured her of His love for her. Nothing had changed, she ached for His gentleness more now than ever and His presence.

When she could, she would take walks feeling led by Him, like His hand was in hers and He would lead her along paths she had never taken. The gentle breezes across her face still made her smile as she remembered back to the very first kiss in the temple all those long years ago.

So much He had taught her and brought her through. From time to time she would think about her husband whom she only knew for seven brief years and her late father and her own mother and now Miriam all

Gone - sleeping now. So many memories and so many tears and confusion and loneliness and yet not for a moment would she change a thing. Every step had taken her deeper into Him, that's all she wanted, and nothing compared with Him.

Anna lifted her eyes and the sun shone so bright, the sky was brilliant blue and empty of clouds. The fragrance of flowers, the Lilies were so strong in the air - that it made her turn to see if He was there. She knelt down and picked a single Lily -for Him.

No one was around. This was the path that the high priest would lead the procession of priests down to the Pool of Siloam, for the Feast of Tabernacles, the festival of Libation. When they would descend the hill to draw the Living Water from that spring before the crowds of thousands each year and carry it all the way back up to the temple where the water would be poured out over the altar.

Anna could hear the sound of water now being splashed around. She was that close, and then the sound of voices, an elderly man and woman were sitting by the spring and stirring the water up with their hands. Anna quietly made her way around them and washed her face with the waters cold and refreshing.

She didn't like to intrude on them in this isolated location and was about to continue walking when the man spoke, and it startled her.

"You are the woman of the temple- Yes, yes, I know of you; are you not the prophetess?" He asked pulling on his wife's arm.

"You are...." He spoke. Then nothing came out.

"Anna" Anna interjected.

"Anna the Prophetess" he said again smiling, "Did you hear that dear? it's her!"

His wife looked quite embarrassed and tried to hush him by placing one finger against his lips.

"The Prophet is here," Anna responded with a humble smile, "My work is done."

The look on their faces spoke louder that than any words could. The couple looked at each other and then grinned.

"Yes, He is!" there seemed to be a long pause before he spoke again-

"We know it for ourselves. Have you heard? He healed our boy; he was born blind." They both stared at the water smiling and lost for a moment in their own thoughts and memories.

"He spat on the ground and made some mud with the saliva and put it on our boys' eyes. He told him to "Go wash in the Pool of Siloam, in this very pool." Their faces were smiling but tears of pure joy formed in both of their eyes, as they recalled that first day, they met the Son of Man through their son being healed.

"Do you know they threw our son out the Synagogue, do you know why? When they asked him who had healed him - He said one thing that he knew - "He once was blind but now he sees"

"He said this is remarkable you don't know where He comes from, yet He opened my eyes, this man they call Jesus." The woman leant against her husband with such love as she spoke the name Jesus.

"We were afraid," he said, "We thought we would be thrown out of the Synagogue and when we were asked, we answered out of fear. He is of age", we said "Ask him."

"But now we know, we met Him, there is No fear in His presence- and we tell everyone He is - who He claims to be, He forgave us, and His Love is...."

His wife reached over to take his hand in hers and finished his sentence for him "His Love is - she breathed in deeply- His Love is Alive"

Anna so desperately wanted to ask what He was like. She wanted them to describe Him to her so she could close her eyes and see Him, but something prevented her, and all she could do was reach out to them with the touch of her hands and thank them for refreshing her.

She slowly turned to leave when the man called her back. "Just one more thing." splashing his hand in the water again, he asked, "Do you understand this?

Anna was unsure what he was doing and meaning as he scooped up the water in his hands and began to drink, then his wife did the same. Anna's eyes never left her face, as he spoke.

"On the last and greatest day of the feast, Jesus stood and said in a loud voice, "If anyone is thirsty, let him come to Me, and drink. Whoever believes in Me as the scriptures has said, streams of Living Water will flow from within him."

Anna fell on her knees and drank deeply of the water in front of her. "You are the Living Water." "You are revealing yourself to us though Your feasts!" Anna muttered under her breath.

"Surely this man is The Prophet," some had called, others said "He is the Christ, and some didn't believe, and the people were divided. I was there, I heard Him." The man spoke with such conviction as he recalled that day of days.

"He is the Light of the world- The Son of God" she whispered, bowing low to the ground, pressing her face into the dust of the earth.

She heard them arise and leave not another word spoken, God had led her on this path to meet these people at this time. She rolled over onto her back and let the warmth of the day touch her deeply.

As Anna stood to leave, she leant over the pool and saw a face - it was so sudden and so beautiful and then gone. All trace of the memory of it gone. "One day," she said, "One day I will see You face to face!"

Anna gently released the Lily and the wind caught it and it landed right in the middle of the spring of Living Waters.

He led her by her hand though unseen back up to the temple. Anna was aware of Him, and she sang quietly to Him, touching the leaves on the trees as she passed along the path, as if touching Him. And He sang through her, His love song.

Then suddenly the words formed in her heart and mind, and she sang them, it was then it all poured out. The very truth of what she had tried to hide even from herself since the day He was born. Would she love His Son the way she had loved Him for most of her life? He was the lover of her soul and her friend and her father. He was everything and now, ever since He had been born, there was doubt. Could the Son of God whom she had prayed to the earth, ever make her feel and touch her heart the way the Father did?

CHAPTER 18

The Message

The room was dark and there was a chill in the air. Anna reached for her Shawl and wrapped it tightly around herself. Something had woken her, her mind was alert and she called to Him, as she lay on her mattress.

Silence and cold remained- she reached out to light her candle, and in the dark, she knocked it to the floor before lighting it. Once again, she called out to Him and waited in the darkness for Him to respond to her.

She slipped out of bed and tried to feel for the candle but could not locate it. "In such a tiny room where could it be?" she wondered.

She used her hands to guide to herself along the wall to the door and opened it, and then she nearly fell backwards at the sight before her. An angel stood right there in front of her, and fear gripped her. He was so much taller than a man, and he shone with such brilliance that Anna froze.

"Be not afraid - I have been sent with a message for you!"

Anna tried to control her breathing as she watched the angel. He put out his hand and peace filled her heart, and with the Light that was coming from him she could see something that sparkled like gold dust, as he moved his hand through the air.

"Fear not, follow me." He spoke with authority and gentleness, and so walking bare feet in the lateness of night, within the temple of God, Anna followed.

He led her to a long corridor she never knew existed and once again fear gripped her, and then as if sensing it himself he turned and spoke.

"Be not afraid Anna- Trust God."

As soon as the words were out of his mouth, the room filled with smoke. He passed something to her and told her to eat. She could no longer stand; all her strength had gone as the Glory of the Lord filled the place. She could not see what he placed in her hand, it was so light and small, and she smiled thinking it could be like the manna they ate in the wilderness.

She popped it in her mouth, and she felt weightless like she was soaring on the wings of the wind. Her eyes were open, and no longer was she in the long corridor or the temple.

And there in front of her—stood the angel.

"Anna"

Someone spoke the Words was it an angel or God - the Words were vibrating inside of her and around her - "This is the message!"

"The Supremacy of Christ. He is the image of the invisible God, the firstborn over-all creation. For by Him all things were created. Things in heaven and on earth, visible and invisible, whether thrones or powers or rulers or authorities, all things were created by Him and for Him."

"He is before all things, and in Him all things hold together. And He is the head of the body, the church. He is the beginning and the first born from among the dead so that in everything He might have the Supremacy. For God was pleased to have all His fullness dwell in Him, and through

Him to reconcile to Himself all things, whether things on earth or things in heaven by making peace through His blood shed on the Cross."

Anna fell so suddenly, like she was falling though the sky, her eyes were closed and heavy as she softly landed, she pulled on the clouds around her and slept, in her bed.

CHAPTER 19

Face to face

The winter was taking its toll on the land scape. The rocky terrain had been covered over in a light layer of snow. The chill in the air seemed to bite through everything. Anna looked down at her hands, age spots were appearing. No longer did they hold the appearance of youth, nor as a young woman, and she knew only too well it was her whole body affected. Her face that had once been beautiful was wrinkled, deep lines around her mouth and on her forehead. Her hair had greyed and thinned, her eyes still held such beauty but saw very little these days. Only from a short distance away could she see. But the one thing she never lost was her keen sense of hearing, even the softest whisper, and she would catch the words.

Anna wrapped the prayer shawl around her even tighter as a strong wind blew so hard it nearly knocked her to the ground. She had a fight to stand. Even harder was walking in her sandals as she slipped on the snowy path. She looked at the old olive trees. How they had changed and grown as she passed them all these years taking this same path to the Mount of Olives.

Walking was so slow, often she would slip. Her knees that were old and bony would come down hard on this layer of snow-covered rocks that cut into her flesh. She gasped, the pain and the cold so hard to break through, but she knew she had to. Today was a good day, it was so infrequent now to have a good day where she was strong enough to leave the temple.

Tears trickled down her face as she noticed the palms of her hands. Blood was flowing from deep lacerations. She wandered back in her mind to the times over the years she had walked this path and sometimes ran like a hind sure footed on the high places. How the flowers had caught her eye. Now all was lost in the winter and the cold.

She loved the temple with all her heart, but there was something about this place that drew her year after year, and so through all the seasons she made the journey when she could.

But this was different. He was here upon the earth and when He was a baby, she had seen Him and there was the time when He was twelve. The Joy, it had brought her, sustained her through all the lonely years.

She had heard about Him, people were always talking about Him now, and once when she was on the mount a large crowd had gathered, she knew it was for Him, to hear Him. And with her own ears although she was so far away from Him that she was prevented from seeing Him at all, she heard Him. "Blessed are you who are poor, for yours is the Kingdom of God," His Voice was loud and powerful full of authority, and it travelled on the wings of the wind so as to reach every open ear all across the mountainside. "Blessed are you who hunger now, for you will be satisfied. Blessed are you who weep now, for you will laugh."

"Oh Lord" Anna thought to herself. "I still laugh with You now."

"Blessed are you when men hate you, when they exclude you and insult you and reject your name as evil, because of the Son of Man,"

He cried out, "Rejoice in that day and leap for Joy, because great is your reward in Heaven. For that is how their fathers treated the prophets."

Somehow, she knew, she was to stay in the background of His life. She had heard about the Miracles and the Words He spoke and how often she longed to be with Him. To catch a glimpse of Him but always she was prevented from being close with Him.

Anna made it to her most favoured place on the mount beside the oldest tree that was gnarled and twisted and yet majestic she looked up to the heavens and cried in her loudest voice "Father, my Father- I love You!"

Suddenly the sun burst through the leaves of the trees and a warmth filled every part of her as she came to her knees in worship.

And then she heard the sound of one walking close towards her. She tried to focus her eyes on His face but the brilliance of Him in that moment was overwhelming and she turned her face away.

"I love you, Anna." Anna fell at His feet, His glorious feet and kissed them. She needed no one to say who it was. His mere presence alone told her what her heart had known of Him. From deep within she heard the Words, "Hear O Israel, the Lord our God is One!!! She smiled and tears cascaded over his feet, and she laughed with pure Joy.

"My Lord You came!" she cried out touching His feet with such love and tenderness. And slowly He bent down and lifted her face to look into her eyes. And He wept!

She looked into the eyes of liquid love, and they poured right into her, and she listened to Him breathing and it was the most wonderful sound and it filled her and all the earth around her.

Anna drew her eyes away from His eyes to His lips and at the same time the scriptures resounded in her, He kisses me with the kisses of His mouth. His lips taste of honey from the honeycomb.

She blushed and brought her own hands to her face to try and hide what she was thinking about Him.

He reached for her hands and laughed so fully and veraciously leaning forward He kissed her on the lips, lingering long enough for her to lose track of time and everything around her disappeared and she was consumed in Him, and He was everything and in everything.

He took her by the hand and lifted her to her feet, smiling with warmth, like He was drinking her in, this very old woman of one hundred and seventeen-years young in that moment.

"Before Abraham was - I AM," He smiled, always aware of what she was thinking.

"Anna, you know why I came!" His gentleness made her weep again, strength from Him flowed through His hands into hers.

"Yes Lord, but if I could...." He placed a finger on her lips to silence the words she would say.

"Trust Me Anna with all your heart, I will rise again. You will see Me again; I tell you the truth."

Anna cried so hard and fell against Him and His arms wrapped around her, and she held Him, clinging tightly to His body for all the lonely years, for all the sadness, for all the times she danced with her pillow imagining Him in her arms. For all the hours of pouring out her heart, praying and singing and listening for Him to share His heart. She held Him for every day in the temple longing for Him, hungering for more of Him. She held Him and breathed the words, "And the Word became flesh," she cried as she recalled the scriptures and what He was to go through and slowly He began to gently move His body swaying from side to side.

"Dance with Me." He whispered and began to move, and she was moulded against His body in a beautiful waltz. He rejoiced over her with singing. It was His own song, His own heart for her alone, personal and intimate as she all these years had bestowed on Him. The love and Joy of Him overflowed her broken heart and she smiled, and He looked down at her, and started to laugh.

"I hear you still have the secret cushion." He teased and Anna laughed. What a beautiful moment with her friend of all these years who knew her thoughts her every treasured memory.

"What do you hear about Me, who do they say I am?" Suddenly His mood had changed as He inquired, He was searching for her eyes, wanting to know.

"My Lord, some say John the Baptist." with that her voice faded away as a distant memory tugged at her heart. In her mind's eye she saw Hephzibah kneeling on the tiles, praying, the scent of the Lord all around her. "Oh, what Joy that woman walked in!" She thought to herself, and He nodded.

"Others say Elijah and still others, Jeremiah or one of the prophets."

"But what about you, who do you say I am?" His smile was lighting up His face and again she had to look away from Him, His beauty was powerful.

Blushing like a young girl, she began to giggle as she looked down at His feet, anything to keep her eyes away from His for this moment. She fumbled with her prayer shawl, doing all she could to avoid answering Him until His hand lifted her chin. and they were face to face.

"Lord, You know all things." The smiles on their faces were brilliant. But His eyes were searching for more, she could feel it in every part of her being.

"Lord, You know I love You." His hand gently touched the side of her face, and a tear fell, and He swept it up with His fingers. He held it to His lips and the words formed against them, "When I was twelve." And He smiled, remembering.

"You are the Holy God of Israel, You are the Almighty, who was and is, and is to come, You are the Messiah, the anointed of God, The Son of the Living God, You are the Christ. You are my life, my love, my reason for living, You are in all things. You are my friend, my poet. You are my God the lover of my soul and my heart. You are the great Shepherd, and I am the sheep of Your pasture. You are my everything. You are my everything!".

For a long time, they just stood face to face in the silence, her fingers wiping the tears as they fell from His eyes. There was a gentle warm breeze that enveloped them both. Forever more I will look into the eyes of Love itself and she knew He heard her thoughts - every one of them.

When she walked away that day down the path away from Him, she could still sense Him watching her. She looked down at her hands that He had just held, and they were healed, she didn't need to look at her knees she knew He had healed them too.

"Thank you, Lord." Anna cried out and she knew deep in her spirit that He had heard all the way to the Throne Room.

And the sound of a voice was carried on the breeze, it came in a whisper, and she caught it and held it in her heart.

"Who is this coming up from the desert, leaning on her lover."

"He remembers!" Anna smiled, as she made her way back to the temple.

"He loves me!"

CHAPTER 20

Cleaning out the house for His father

It was the feast of Unleavened Bread just before Passover. Anna lay upon her bed in her windowless room, frail and weak. Something was stirring in her spirit; a heavy weight was upon her. And with wisdom of the years, she knew it was not of her but about Him. She would wake often now in such despair, with tears that flowed without her understanding why.

As she lay in her darkened room with her candle burning dimly, memories flooded her heart, and she saw herself as a girl in the home of her parents. She and her mother would search through the house for any leaven. Every year it was like a game they would play, with every other Jewish family doing the same. It was a commandment of God that on the first day of the feast all the leaven had to be out of every home.

She recalled her mother hiding some that they could find as her father and her searched through the house with a candle and gently with a feather they would sweep the leaven onto a wooden spoon and then they would wrap it all in a linen cloth and take it outside the house. And the following day there would be a bonfire and all the families would watch it burn.

As she lay there, the Holy Spirit spoke into her heart and revealed to her the mystery of her memories. The candle was the Word of God, leaven was sin that must be cast out of the house. The feather was The Holy Spirit, and the wooden spoon was the cross. "No" Anna sobbed holding her hands to her ears as if to stop hearing the Words He was revealing to her. And the linen cloth and Anna knew, is what He will be buried in. And the fire was the Wrath of God as He paid the price for all man outside the city gates.

She lay on her bed like a baby in a fetal position, sobbing uncontrollably because it was soon, she just knew it. Suddenly the candle in her room became much brighter and she knew He was near; she could sense Him. He was somewhere in the temple or the outer courts.

She sat up and placed her hand flat on the wall, knowing He was there and very stirred up in His spirit. Something powerful was taking place.

Suddenly she started to pray words flowing in the spirit and then it came from her lips, but she knew without any doubt she was praying what He was saying with such earnestness and power. "My house shall be called a house of prayer for all nations, but you have made it a den of robbers!"

She stood in the silence her hand touching the wall but in the spirit with all her heart she was touching Him, and He had had just cleansed His Father's house of its leaven and she understood.

"Zeal for Your house will consume You."

CHAPTER 21

Anointed with oil twice

Six days before the Passover Jesus arrived at Bethany, where His friends Lazarus and his two sisters lived. A dinner was served in Jesus' honour. Martha served, whilst Lazarus was among those reclining at the table with Him. Then Mary took about a pint of pure Nard, an expensive perfume, and she poured it on Jesus' feet and wiped His feet with her hair and the house was filled with the fragrance of the perfume.

When Anna overheard this, she knew what was happening. God's lamb was being inspected for blemishes as they did each Passover, and the High Priest would pour oil over the feet of the lamb. Days of inspections would take place, so it didn't surprise her when she heard that two days before the Passover at the home of Simon the Leper a woman came with an alabaster jar of very expensive perfume made of pure Nard. She broke the jar and poured the perfume on His head. He was once again fulfilling every feast and yet not one who spoke of it to her or who were present with Him, saw the connection. Even with His powerful words that were repeated around the temple gates.

He said, "The poor you will always have with you, and you can help them anytime you want, but you will not always have Me."

Some of those present had been saying indignantly to one another, "Why this waste of perfume?" "It could have been sold for more than a year's wages and the money given to the poor." They had rebuked her sharply.

Anna hid her face from those gathered around telling the story as they spoke of His next words. "She did what she could. She poured perfume on My body beforehand to prepare for My burial. I tell you the truth, wherever the gospel is preached throughout the world. What she has done will also be told, in memory of her."

Anna scurried away like a wounded animal and cried. It was too close, too real, and she knew He would die. And something else rose up in her, an emotion she has never had to deal with before. She was jealous, of the relationship all these people had with Him. They walked with Him, and sat with Him, and she cried, "I never got to anoint You." She wiped her tears with her shawl and felt so sorry for herself, no - one knew her. She would never be remembered, all the lonely years, she would never be thought of no one would know, that she Knew Him, that she prayed Him to this place, that she loved Him."

CHAPTER 22

Passover - Singing Psalm 113-118

Anna sat alone on the floor of her room with the Passover plate pushed away from her, untouched. She cried and cried as she sang the "Hallel" her favorite one and yet at this moment so difficult to sing.

"I love the Lord for He heard my voice; He heard my cry for mercy. Because He turned His ear to me, I will call on Him as long as I live."

She picked up the pillow from the bed and hugged it tightly against herself as she imagined He would be singing it at this time, but not alone. He would be with His followers, His disciples - those closest to Him.

"The cords of death entangled me, the anguish of the grave came upon me, I was overcome by trouble and sorrow- then I called on the Name of the Lord, O Lord save me!"

"The Lord is gracious and righteous; our God is full of compassion. The Lord protects the simple hearted; when I was in great need, He saved me."

"Be at rest once more O my soul, for the Lord has been good to you."

"For You O Lord have delivered my soul from death, my eyes from tears, my feet from stumbling, that I may walk before the Lord in the land of the living."

"I believed therefore I said, "I am greatly afflicted. And in my dismay, I said, "all men are liars"

"How can I repay the Lord for all His goodness to me?"

"I will lift up the Cup of Salvation and call on the Name of the Lord. I will fulfil my vows to the Lord in the presence of all His people."

'Precious in the sight of the Lord is the death of His saints. O Lord truly I am your servant, the son of Your maid servant, You have freed me from my chains."

"I will sacrifice a thank offering to you and call on the Name of the Lord. I will fulfill my vows to the Lord in the presence of all His people, in the courts of the house of the Lord, in your midst O Jerusalem. Praise the Lord."

Suddenly a strange peace overflowed Anna, and she tried to imagine Jesus and what He was thinking, how He was feeling. Somehow as frightened as she was, from the encounter they had shared such a short time ago, she could not imagine Him frightened. He would have set His face like flint and headed on to this very moment. A thought came to her that He may even be delighted to be sharing this very Passover, that it may have been with great longing before He suffers.

She wondered at the Words He would speak on this last night and tears flowed down her cheeks again. Son of God - Son of man. "Did those with Him know what would take place, did they believe, did they have any understanding of who He really is and where He is from?" Anna stood to her feet feeling restless as she thought, "And what He is about to go through."

Anna wrapped her shawl tightly around her shoulders and walked out of her room. She had no idea where to go or what to do with herself, she just knew she could not sit still. With all her heart she wanted to cry out to her Father and beg for this not to take place, but that was why He was here.

CHAPTER 23

His Last Prayer the Night He was Betrayed

Anna headed out into the night and walked with such a heaviness of heart. The moon was lighting up the sky and she was thankful for the stars and all the beauty that was displaying the Glory of God.

She remembered walking along this path at this time, The Lords Passover all those years ago. Year after year and weeping and being drawn to the place that even now her heart was drawing her too. Not since He had come had she taken this walk - in such despair and yet such a hunger to reach the place - He was leading her to the garden.

Anna walked on with tears washing down her face, the weightiness of the truth drew her to her knees. She stayed on the rocky path and noticed the low branches of the trees had hidden her from view.

Softly Anna started to sing as the wind blew against her face.

"The stone the builders rejected has become the cornerstone and the Lord has done this - and it is marvelous in our eyes." Anna bowed low to the ground her face touching the dirt and groaned with such pain from deep within her.

"This is the day the Lord has made; O let us rejoice and be glad in it."

Crouched over she kept on singing, her voice coming out like a broken whisper; the Psalm all of Israel would be singing.

"You are my God, and I will give You thanks, You are my God and I will exalt You. Give thanks to the Lord, for He is good; His love endures forever."

Anna sniffled and breathed so deeply, sobbing and drowning out the sound in her prayer shawl. Suddenly the sound of a voice filled the air. It was Him, and she stayed bowed low as He and His disciples approached the path near her. She listened to Him and heard Him pray as He walked.

"My prayer is not that You take them out of the world but that You protect them from the evil one. They are not of this world, even as I am not of it. Sanctify them by the truth; Your Word, is truth. As You sent Me into the world, I have sent them into the world. For them I sanctify Myself, that they too may be truly sanctified."

The group of them seemed to stop there for a moment, Anna was afraid to even take a breath, she could see their feet and knew instinctively which were His. How she would long to reach out and touch Him. And then He moved, and the feet followed.

"My prayer is not for them alone. I pray also for those who will believe in Me through their message, that all of them may be one, Father, just as You are in Me and I am in You."

Anna heard the love in His voice as He spoke the word. "Father" she could imagine flowers opening in bloom, and the stars shining that much brighter, the mighty waves roaring at the love with which He spoke the Name, "Father."

"May they also be in Us so that the world may believe that You have sent Me. I have given them the Glory that You gave Me, that they may be One as We are One; I in them and You in Me. May they be brought to complete unity to let the world know that You sent Me and have loved them, even as You have loved Me."

"Father, I want those you have given Me to be with Me where I am, and to see My Glory, The Glory You have given Me because You loved Me before the creation of the world."

"Righteous Father, though the world does not know You, I know You, and they know that You have sent Me. I have made You known to them and will continue to make You known to them in order that the love You have for Me may be in them, and that I Myself may be in them."

When He had finished praying, Jesus left with His disciples and crossed the Kidron Valley. On the other side was the Olive grove and He and His disciples went into it.

Anna stood to her feet overwhelmed with hearing His blessed prayer to His Beloved Father. She herself slowly followed in His footsteps across the Kidron Valley, the very Brook where in the days of King Hezekiah, they removed the altars in Jerusalem and cleared away the incense altars and threw them into the Kidron Valley. It was Passover. It was the Feast of Unleavened Bread. Cleaning out the Temple for The Lord!

CHAPTER 24

In the Garden

As Anna made her way deeper into the garden, she saw them, fast asleep leaning against the olive trees, only Jesus was not with them. Quietly she crept through the undergrowth, about a stone's throw beyond them and saw Him. He was kneeling and praying. Over and over, she heard Him cry out in such anguish, "Father; if You are willing, take this cup from Me, yet not My will, but Yours be done."

Anna bit into the prayer cloth to stop herself from calling out, His body was glistening and with the moon light shining on His face she could see His sweat had become like drops of blood falling to the ground.

Anna knelt behind a large old olive tree as silent tears flowed. She wanted with all her heart to run to Him and hold Him and to hide Him from that which was to come, but an unseen force held her to the ground, and she knew its name "Love."

There was only one thing she could do and after all these long years she knew without doubt something she did well. And for a moment then she smiled as she looked over at Him.

Anna silently prayed for Him in the strength and the power of His Spirit. Suddenly He stood and walked back to His men, and He Found them sleeping. Anna heard Him ask "Why are you sleeping? Get up and pray so that you will not fall into temptation. Again, He left them and knelt down a stone throw away, this time even closer to Anna. And she wondered "Did He know, she was there?"

"Father, if You are willing, take this cup from Me, yet not My will but Yours be done."

And on and on He prayed in deep anguish His heart full of sorrow and on and on Anna prayed in deep anguish her heart full of sorrow. And she remembered this bitter place and the torment in her soul she had walked through it - before Him - and now all these years later she walked through it with Him. "Jesus," she whispered, "I'm here."

He was crying now, no more words and Anna desperately wanted to do something, comfort Him somehow.

"Father" she whispered "Father, do something - help Him." It was too much to bear watching Him go through this. She felt like she was going to break open inside.

And then right in front of her eyes, an angel from heaven appeared to Him and strengthened Him. And being in such anguish He prayed even more earnestly.

Returning the third time, He said to them, "Are you still sleeping and resting? Enough! The hour has come, look the Son of Man is betrayed into the hands of sinners. Rise! Let us go! Here comes My betrayer."

CHAPTER 25

Jesus Arrested

Whilst He was still speaking a crowd came up armed with swords and clubs, and a man, one of the twelve was leading them. They were holding torches and lanterns - the night was lit up like day. He approached Jesus, but Jesus asked him, "Judas, are you betraying the Son of Man with a kiss?"

Jesus knowing what was going to happen to Him asked them, "Who is it you want?"

"Jesus of Nazareth", they replied.

"I am He" Jesus said, and with that they drew back and fell to the ground.

Again, He asked them "Who is it you want?"

And they said "Jesus of Nazareth"

"I told you I am He, if you are looking for Me, then let these men go."

Then one of the men who had a sword drew it and struck the High priest's servant, cutting off his right ear.

Jesus commanded the man, "Put your sword away! Shall I not drink the cup the Father has given Me?"

"Do you think I cannot call on My Father, and He will at once put at My disposal more that twelve legions of angels? But how then would the scripture be fulfilled that it must happen this way?"

"No more of this!" and He touched the man's ear and healed him.

Anna was frozen to the spot in terror - the hour had come, and she was grateful to her hiding spot behind the olive tree. There were so many men, so much fear in the air.

Then Jesus said to the chief priests, the officers of the temple guard, and the elders who had come for Him,

"Am I leading a rebellion, that you have come with swords and clubs? Every day I was with you in the temple courts, and you did not lay a hand on Me, but this is your hour - when darkness reigns, but all this has taken place that the writings of the prophets might be fulfilled." All the disciples deserted Him and fled.

Then the detachment of soldiers with its commander and the Jewish officials arrested Jesus. They bound Him, and all Anna understood was He never resisted. He was allowing everything. She saw His face as the light shone upon it, His face was full of love, not fear - even when they struck Him - all she saw was love.

A numbness and a helplessness washed over her as she remained in that place, staring up at the sky, not a prayer - no song - not a tear – silence.

The Lamb of God - who takes away the sin of the world was now being led away to die. Anna looked at the place where they had all been and now it was darkness, she could see the faintest glow down at the foot of the mount from their lanterns and she knew not what to do with herself.

CHAPTER 26

The New Covenant

Hours passed and Anna had not moved from her hiding place in the garden of Gethsemane. She was cold and slowly stood to her feet and made the journey down the mount. The sun had risen, but it was not warm. She ached all over from the night air.

Just before she reached the bottom something drew her attention, and she turned her head to see a lily just a little off the path. Though she slipped on the rocks she still managed to pick it, and just holding it in her hands made her cry- she thought of Him.

Where would He be now, what would they be doing to Him. How much was He to suffer, before He was to die? She headed to the temple the one place she always felt safe and closest to Him as she lay herself down on the tiles.

Tears flowed and she thought of every wonderful memory she had - each time she had encountered Him- the way He spoke to her and laughed with her - and corrected her and taught her, before she had even seen His face.

"You are a man-You came as a man- flesh and blood." she looked at her own hands and remembered His hands touching her face, drying her tears. "God- how can You do this?" she sobbed as she turned her hands over and imagined His hand nailed to the cross. She dropped her hand to her side and stood angry that she could not stop this. All she could do was cry, her insides hurt from crying so long and hard. She started to pace backwards and forwards and then a powerful urge to pray came upon her.

She prayed in the spirit all the morning through pacing and weeping, was it for her, or for Him, all she knew was she driven by a force stronger than herself. At times she cried out so violently and fell to the ground. In her strength alone she could never get through this day.

Suddenly Anna had such a desire to be with Him, to help Him somehow, so He wouldn't be alone.

"Where would they take Him?" she wondered again; I have to find Him. Standing to her feet she felt lightheaded and dizzy, she swallowed repeatedly, fighting the nausea. One tiny step then another - till she could reach a wall and lean against it.

Outside the temple the sun had well risen, it was late in the morning, and she knew there was a place that He might be- the Palace the Governor's official residence.

On and on she walked stopping frequently to lean against something to catch her breath and wait for the light headedness to pass. And then there it was, and fear gripped her again as she climbed the stairs and headed into the open doors of the palace.

There were soldiers standing around and talking as she walked past them and even looked into their faces. No one spoke a word to her, or even looked at her like he could see her. Something strange was happening, and now she knew the name of the place she was looking for "The Praetorium" The place they took their prisoners to be flogged.

Nothing prepared Anna for what her eyes beheld as she stood at the entrance to the room. She let out a deep guttural cry as she got down on her knees and shook - her whole body shook with shock.

It was blood - all over the tiles- pools of blood - His Blood she just knew. This was the whipping post that He was tied to. Anna crawled along the tiles, her body still shaking, and imagined Him willingly offering up His body, as the sacrifice.

She imagined Him sliding on the tiles as His blood formed puddles around His feet. She looked up and saw the chains that would have held His wrists and knew He would have stayed without them. It was just so much blood, and then she saw the tables that held the instruments of torture.

Even with her poor eyes sight, she could see the blood and bits of flesh that had caught on the chards of bone along the whip.

It all became too much and inside of her she screamed.

"I wasn't worth it, I wasn't worth it, I wasn't worth it." She rocked back and forwards deeply distressed.

She looked at His precious Blood and knew from scripture, "The Life is in the Blood, He had poured out His Blood and given His life to the world."

Over and over, she repeated to herself, that she wasn't worth it, that it was too high a price, crying and screaming on the inside until she had nothing left and lay silently on the tiles beside His Blood.

It was then she heard it, a still soft whisper, and she closed her eyes to listen as His Words became part of her.

"You prepare a table before me in the presence of my enemies,"

"For the Bread of God is He who comes down from Heaven and gives life to the world. If anyone eats of this Bread, he will live forever. This Bread is My flesh, which I will give for the life of the world. I tell you the truth unless you eat the flesh of the Son of Man and drink His Blood, you have no life in you. Whoever eats My flesh and drinks My Blood has Eternal Life, and I will raise him up at the last day. For My flesh is real food and My Blood is real drink. Whoever eats My flesh and drinks My Blood abides in Me, and I in Him."

"Just as the Living Father sent Me, and I live because of the Father, so the one who feeds on Me will live because of Me."

"The Words I have spoken to you are Spirit and they are Life"

"Take eat, this is My body broken for you."

"Take drink,"

"This is My Blood of the New Covenant which is poured out for many for the forgiveness of sins."

CHAPTER 27

The Lily laid at the foot of the Cross

In total exhaustion Anna dragged herself outside into the fresh air. With every breath in her body, she wanted to make her way to Golgotha the place of the skull. She longed so much for a drink after shedding so many tears her thirst and grief were getting the better of her.

A man she did not know came to her and offered her help, by guiding her gently toward the temple. She tried so hard to resist but her strength was gone, and he carried her the last part of the way as she cried in his arms.

He lay her down on the mattress in her room and Anna whispered to him, through closed eyes, because she could no longer keep them open. "Take this to Jesus."

And he disappeared.

CHAPTER 28

Laid in the Tomb

Anna lay on the bed in a state of pure exhaustion. She never slept - though her eyes remained closed. Her mind kept replaying what she saw and heard in the Praetorium. The colour red was everywhere.

Anna arose from the bed and wondered how she had managed to come back to her room. She was still lightheaded and drank deeply of the water jar by her bed. She wondered what the time was, and whether He was still alive.

As she made her way to the temple doors, she was aware of people gathered all around, praying, talking, something had happened, the mood of the people was charged and excited.

She drew near to listen, and without even thinking the words came out her mouth. "Tell me where is He?"

Silence followed as they all turned to look at her, quite surprised that she didn't know.

One bold young man spoke up and then another, and then another, everyone had something so amazing to share.

"He cried out from the cross, "I am thirsty" and a jar of wine vinegar was there, so they soaked a sponge in it, put the sponge on a stalk of the hyssop plant and lifted it to Jesus lips. When He had received the drink,

Jesus said, "It is finished."

"Jesus called out with a loud voice, "Father, into Your hands I commit My spirit."

"With that He bowed His head, and He breathed His last."

"The curtain of the temple was torn in two from top to bottom. And when the centurion who stood there in from of Jesus, heard His cry and saw how He died, he said, "Surely this man was the Son of God!"

"The soldiers came and broke the legs of the first man who had been crucified with Jesus, and then those of the other."

"They did this for it was the day of preparation, and the next day was to be a special Sabbath. The Jews did not want the bodies left on the crosses during the Sabbath, so they asked Pilate to have the legs broken and taken down."

Anna nearly fell but one of the young men caught her and she leaned against him. It was so hard to hear, tears cascaded down her cheeks.

"But when they came to Jesus, and found that He was already dead, they did not break His legs,"

"Instead, one of the soldiers pierced Jesus side with a spear, bringing a sudden flow of blood and water."

"These things happened so that the scriptures would be fulfilled. "Not one of His bones will be broken' "and as another scripture says, "They will look on the one they have pierced."

"At the sixth hour darkness came over the whole land until the ninth hour, for the sun stopped shining, and at that ninth hour Jesus cried out in a loud voice, "My God, My God, why have You forsaken Me?" Anna wept.

They all stopped for a moment to see if she was strong enough to continue, and slowly she regained her composure. Though the tears continued to flow, Anna nodded that she was alright.

"Joseph of Arimathea, a prominent member of the council, who was himself waiting for the Kingdom of God went boldly to Pilate and asked for Jesus body. Pilate was surprised to find Jesus already dead. With Pilates permission he came and took the body away. He was accompanied by Nicodemus."

Anna wondered to herself whether he was the same Nicodemus she had met in the outer courts, after his visit with Jesus at night alone?

"He brought a mixture of Myrrh and aloes, about seventy-five pounds."

"They took Jesus body the two of them and wrapped it with the spices, in strips of linen. At the place where Jesus was crucified there was a garden and, in the garden, a new tomb, in which no one had ever been laid. Because it was Jewish day of preparation, and since the tomb was nearby, they laid Jesus there.

The women who had come with Jesus from Galilee followed Joseph and saw the tomb and how His body was laid in it. They went home now to prepare spices and perfumes. But would rest in obedience to the commandment regarding the Sabbath.

CHAPTER 29

Resurrection

Anna had not slept, nor eaten. She was overwhelmed with grief and so overcome with sorrow. She never knew crying hurt -the pain caused by her deep sobbing, was unlike anything she had ever experienced. She banged her tiny fists into the hard tiles.

This was what it had all been about, this is why He had come, and she had prayed Him to this very earth, she had loved Him, and ached for His presence. And yet in His darkest hour, with the weight of the sins of the world laid upon Him. She had left Him alone.

"How could she ever forgive herself?" The anger rose up inside of her directed at herself, such frustration and disappointment in her weakness and frailty.

She knelt on the hard tiles, without the soft cushion, to pad her bony knees. She rocked back and forth in such despair. Wanting no comfort or peace for the torment in her heart and mind.

He was gone. Buried in a tomb.

Tears ran down her face and she moaned with the pain. The emptiness she felt within her heart, was consuming her every moment.

He had died and she had not been there. He had taken His last breath and she had not heard it. She had not seen His eyes or brought Him any comfort, she never said goodbye.

Slowly she crawled herself off the floor and with sheer determination took each step towards the doors of the temple. The Sabbath was over, and she could go to the place they had laid Him. It was so early; the light of morning had not broken through. If she had not known the rocky path so well, she never would have found it with her poor eyesight.

There was a strong breeze blowing and her candle would not stay lit. The breeze stung her eyes that were already blinded by tears. And then she heard the sound of women talking and crying, they must have been on a path close to the one she was on. And then the sounds faded as they walked faster along the path ahead.

There was a violent earthquake.

Anna stumbled and fell and as she tried to stand, she knew her leg would not support her weight. With all her strength she lay down and pulled herself along the path with her arms. Continuously she had to stop as her breathing became laboured.

The sun was well risen now and sweat droplets were forming on her brow, and on and on she pulled herself along the rocky path, the blood was flowing from her elbows to her wrists and the palms of her hands were raw open wounds.

Anna stumbled slowly along the path into the garden, and without looking up she heard the sound of voices. A man and a woman's voice. Anna lifted her head and saw what looked like a gardener by the linen he was wearing, and he had asked the woman, "Why she was weeping, who was she looking for?" His concern for her seemed real like it mattered to Him, almost like it pleased Him, that she was so grieved for whoever it was.

"If you have carried Him from here, tell me where you have put Him, and I will go and get Him!!" It was a desperate plea, Anna had no idea who the distressed woman was, but she knew, it had to be about Jesus. Jesus body must be missing. And she felt like the wind had been knocked out of her as she looked toward the tomb, she could see the stone had been rolled away from the entrance.

She took no breath in the silence, as her mind scanned back to Adam and Eve in the garden. And the Lord God came walking through the trees in the cool of the day calling and looking for them. And His heart cry as He called out "Woman what hast thou done?" She was nameless and everything was lost. And they were cast out from the garden, from the Tree of Life, from the Blessing, the wages of sin were death.

One word, one word was spoken and both women knew who He was, He said "Mary."

He had restored All things in that one moment! Death had lost its sting. Jesus had given His life to the world - Eternal Life! The Father had restored Him to life by the Power of the Holy Spirit. Anna looked back to the tomb where the stone had been rolled away, the amazing price He paid to redeem us.

Anna lay on the ground weeping and then realized something had happened to her, she looked at her hands, and then her wrists, and elbows and stretched out her leg. Her tears drowned out the sound of them speaking, as she marveled at the healing, she had received just by being in the garden with Him.

She came to her knees and beheld Him standing, a short distance from her. He was smiling- He was alone now. And her eyes could see Him clearly.

"You did it" She cried out, and He walked slowly toward her, and she could hear the sound of Him breathing, and she breathed in the sound and cried, with excitement and sorrow and guilt and love.

"I'm so sorry, I'm so sorry, I wasn't there, can You ever...." He placed a finger near her lips to silence her words.

"Your every tear was a love song and your every prayer a fragrance. There was not one tear cried for Me or ever will be, that did not touch Me.!"

"My Lord, but I......."

"Were with Me! You left a Lily at the foot of My cross, you knelt down -you cried all alone for Me, but your heart was kneeling at the foot of My cross."

"But how, how did You know it was from me?"

"I know you, Anna, I know you." He smiled and it lit up Anna's heart, like the sun and the moon He had promised to be for her for all eternity.

"Jesus!"

And face to face they simply stood watching the other- eyes fixed, hearts open. He heard her thoughts like waves breaking on the shore one after another, thanking Him, loving Him - wanting to touch Him - and for the first time she heard His thoughts, and they drank in the silent conversation they had with each other's hearts.

"I will be a star for You."

He shook His head. He looked as uncomfortable as she was, with not being able to touch yet, as He had not yet ascended to His Father-

"Those who turn many to righteousness will be like the stars in the sky." she persisted, like an excited child.

Again, He shook His head. "No - there's something I want to show you- Heaven." He smiled.

Anna interrupted Him without meaning to, she talked over the top of Him.

"I will meet my Father," she said with such longing and Jesus looked away, was it pain in His eyes, she wondered?

"Don't you know Me. Have I been with you for so long now and you do not know Me?" His tone told her He was teasing her. "Anyone who has seen Me has seen the Father. Don't you believe that I am in the Father and the Father is in Me?"

Anna laughed and threw her head back with such Joy. "I know You, from the very beginning- I know You." she beamed.

"Anna, I want to thank you - through it all You clung to Me. I go now to prepare a place for you."

"I shall surely dwell in the house of My Lord," Anna burst out with pure joy, "Forever," He smiled and laughed with her. Anna watched until He faded from her view, in the twinkling of an eye, He disappeared.

And she shouted His Name - for all of heaven and earth to hear! "You passed Your test," she called with such delight walking briskly back to the temple, like a young calf released from the stalls - more in love than ever.

CHAPTER 30

One last look at the Temple

It was quiet as she returned to the temple and yet inside, she was anything but peaceful and still- her excitement was explosive. She giggled using the tiles on the floor like a game as she made her way to her room. The room seemed even smaller now, stuffy and dark and yet all these long years it been such a luxury for her. It held so many memories and she smiled and grabbed the pillow from her bed and began to dance with it as she had all those years imagining it was Him. Remembering the time, He as a young boy had laid His head on it and gently slept in this room.

She remembered her favorite experience with Him, it was after He had withdrawn His presence from her all those long months whilst He tested her. When He came back that morning and filled the room with Light and Joy. So much joy. She reached out and touched the walls and knelt down to give her thanks to the One who had given her a lifetime of Himself.

She rose to leave smiling and laughing knowing deep in her heart she would never be back in this room again. She closed the door on the way out and walked like on air toward her place on the tiles that she met with Him that first day.

She sat on her bottom, on the soft pillow, no longer hiding it and began to sing to Him.

"My Beloved spoke and said to me, rise up My love, My fair one, and come away- for lo the winter is past, the rain is over and gone. The flowers appear on the earth: The time of singing has come, and the voice of the turtle dove is heard in our land. The fig tree puts forth her green figs, and the vines with the tender grapes give a good smell.

Rise up, My love, My fair one and come away."

CHAPTER 31

Taken Home

The priests gathered around her body and wept as a young man in his early twenties came from behind a column and spoke about the radiance of her. He said he heard her singing, saw her smiling, her eyes were focused on something right in front of her. She was filled with light and the gentlest breeze was blowing against her face. Her veil was blown away from her and then as if someone was there, she lay back in..." He paused for a moment as he saw again in his mind's eye, that last moment.

"It was as if she lay back - in the arms of someone, and...and..." He started to shake, something extraordinary had happened right before his eyes, that he was having trouble coming to terms with.

His voice wavered as he continued, shock was setting in and he collapsed to his knees.

"I saw a Lily- and then it was ... placed in her hand.... no one was there." The priests closed her eyes. Her smile remained and even as she was laid in linen- the Lily could not be removed from her hand. Some supernatural force prevented anyone from taking it away from her.

"Does anyone know who she was?" The young man asked watching as they carefully wrapped her in linen.

"Anna - the Prophetess, the daughter of Phanuel of the tribe of Asher- she was married once for seven years and when her husband died, she came to the temple and fasted and prayed and never left the temple." "A Holy woman?" the young man questioned.

I wonder what her story was. The man thought to himself as he left the temple, he walked out into the sunshine along the path leading to the Mount of Olives. People were everywhere talking laughing, and then he heard it, someone shouted, and it penetrated deep within his soul, and he believed the words.

"He is risen - Jesus the Christ is risen. Mary said she saw Him!"

And the mantle of the Prophet fell upon the young man as he was led by the spirit to search out this Anna and the God whom she knew- Jesus...

"I will seek You with all my heart and I will find YOU," he declared as he knelt on the Mount of Olives, his eyes lifted to the heavens. Echoing in his mind was the last word he heard the Holy woman Anna speak, it was like they were face to face as she spoke His Name.

"Jesus!"

This was no ordinary day!

ABOUT THE AUTHOR

Carol Anderson loves the LORD, she loves reading His Word and sharing His Word. Her greatest delight is knowing she is in His presence; in worship, in prayer, even just walking along the river and talking with Him.

The Lord Jesus truly is her all in all, and she really enjoys His love as He has been with her through sorrows, grief, so much loss and He has turned it all around and given her much beauty and blessed her life in so many ways.

The Holy Spirit has been her wonderful teacher, incredible friend and He makes her smile and dance for joy. He completes her.

Her passion is for deeper intimacy with God for herself and for others. He is more than a word on a page, He is the fullness of joy!

He is her love story.

www.ingramcontent.com/pod-product-compliance
Lightning Source LLC
LaVergne TN
LVHW091007080826
845145LV00003B/1164